Praise for Copper Skin, Oaken Lungs

"Part *Silo*, part *Annihilation* and part *The Walking Dead*, but with fantasy and magic and fresh worldbuilding all of its own, this book is a creepy, sinister, surreal, heartwarming yet heartbreaking tale of seeking light from the dark. I loved it."
—**Ed Crocker**, author of The Everlands Trilogy.

"This compact fantasy novel overflows with the kind of deep, immersive worldbuilding one usually finds in five hundred-plus page doorstoppers."
—**J. Patricia Anderson**, author of *Your Blood and Bones*.

"Strong female leads, magic, and an all-consuming world, this story has it all."
—**Molly Macabre**, author of *Dark Bloom* and *What Comes Before*.

Copper Skin, Oaken Lungs

Adam Bassett

eBook ISBN: 979-8-9909819-6-6
Paperback ISBN: 979-8-9909819-7-3
Audiobook ISBN: 979-8-9909819-8-0

Cover Illustration by Silvia Gorchakova (@gorchart)
Cover Design by Adam Bassett
Interior Illustrations & Formatting by Adam Bassett

Developmental Editing by Ed Crocker
Copy Editing by Qilanna Quinn

Contents

For all those who seek a light in times of darkness.

About Content
Warnings

Copper Skin, Oaken Lungs is intended for mature audiences. While I would consider it appropriate for most ages, details on its content warnings can be found at the end of this book or on adamcbassett.com.

Dramatis Personæ

The main cast & citizens of The Old Town

Anna *(ah-na)*: Younger daughter of Oļegs, apprentice of Oļegs.

Aleks *(ah-lecks)*: Grocer & apothecary.

Beatrice *(bee-a-treece)*: Wife to Lord Mayor Dmitraj & baker.

Bruno *(broo-noe)*: Brewer.

Dmitraj *(dmee-trai)*: Husband to Beatrice, Lord Mayor.

Ešlija *(esh-lee-yah)*: Member of the town guard, master to her son Gustavs.

Gustavs *(goo-stavs)*: Son of Ešlija, apprentice of Ešlija.

Graudiņš *(grou-dinzh)*: Farmer, master to Justīne.

Ievan *(ee-vuhn)*: Blacksmith.

Justīne *(yu-stee-nuh)*: Eldest daughter of Oļegs, apprentice of Graudiņš.

Krišs *(kree-shs)*: Butcher, father to Teodor.

Lilija *(li-li-yah)*: Rancher.

Niklāvs *(nee-klayvs)*: Member of the Lord Mayor's personal guard.

Oļegs *(oe-likhs)*: Engineer, master to his daughter Anna, father to Justīne.

Pūka *(poo-kah)*: Graudiņš cat, cunning hunter of mice and small birds.

Sofija *(soh-fee-yah)*: Surgeon and singer, elder sister to Staņislavs.

Staņislavs *(stan-ee-slavs)*: Carpenter and singer, younger brother to Sofija.

Teodor *(tee-oh-door)*: Member of the town guard, son of Krišs.

Zigmārs *(zeeg-marz)*: Younger son of Lord Mayor Dmitraj and Beatrice.

Dzevrs (Deceased) *(zev-ers)*: Eldest son of Lord Mayor Dmitraj and Beatrice.

Karīna (Deceased) *(kah-ree-nah)*: Engineer, with moderate skill in magic.

Monika (Deceased) *(Mah-nik-ah)*: Mage.

Timurs (Deceased) *(tee-murs)*: Engineer, master to Oļegs and Karīna.

Glossary

Select words and phrases

Common Terms

Atstrumeter *(at-stroo-meter)*: Machines, mostly made of copper, that emit a barrier which repels the maalkonis. They run on solar power and are supported by an alternator. When placed in a row, they can create invisible protective walls or domes. Occasionally referred to as *atstrus (at-stroos)*.

Dādi *(dah-di)*: The Ļaodil's term for "father." *Padādi (pah-dah-di)* is the common term for "stepfather."

Ļaodil *(lah-dihl)*: The people of The Old Town refer to themselves collectively as the Ļaodil.

Maalkonis *(mahl-kohn-iss)*: The dark cloud surrounding The Old Town which appears to consume everything it touches.

Mama *(mah-mah)*: The Ļaodil's term for "mother." *Pamaman (pah-mah-mahn)* is the common term for "step-mother."

Meita *(may-tah)*: "Daughter," as a term of endearment.

Mortežs *(mort-esh)*: The name of the dead forests in the *maalkonis*.

Phrases

Lavekzīme *(lavehk-zeem)*: A phrase of good luck, often wishing it upon others.

Malsavekzīme *(mahl-savehk-zeem)*: A phrase of bad luck, often calling a thing, situation, or event bad luck.

Times of Day

With the *maalkonis* forming a dark dome around The Old Town, the Ļaodil have a slightly different perception on time and the passing of it. A day is broken up into four quarters, determined by the position of the sun. Most quarters have an associated meal and prayer.

Prausme *(prows-may)*: Refers to the time of day when citizens of The Old Town break their fast and offer their first prayers for the day, often shortly after walking up. When referring to the time of day specifically, separate from the meal or prayer, it is more commonly referred to as *First Dim*, referring to the first of the sun's dim light.

Repukdau *(ree-puk-dow)*: Refers to the time of day when people eat lunch and offer their second prayers for the day. When referring to the time of day specifically, separate from this, it is more commonly referred to as *Midday*.

Vekrēla *(vek-ray-la)*: Refers to the time of day when people eat dinner and offer their final prayers for the day. When referring to the time of day specifically, separate from this, it is more commonly referred to as *Last Dim*, referring to the last of the sun's light.

Noctis *(nock-tis)*: There is no nighttime prayer, so *Noctis* generally only refers to the time of day between *first* and *last dim*. At its darkest hour people often refer to the time as *Midnoct*.

Numerals

Viens *(vyens)*: One
Divi *(di-vi)*: Two
Trīs *(tree-s)*: Three

THE OLD TOWN
The Hills
The Farmhouse
Olegs' House
The Guardhouse
The Old Cathedral

I

A ceaseless din filled the air as the atstrumeters' copper gears spun. Dozens of the machines were mounted along the wall that surrounded The Old Town, humming in unison, holding back the world's blight. Justīne and her little sister scaled the wall, using missing and protruding bricks to cling onto it. When she reached the top, Justīne extended a hand down to Anna. She took it, and Justīne pulled back, lifting her up. They both collapsed on the narrow walkway, breathing deeply.

The Old Town lay entirely within the wall's embrace, its façade blending in with the brick and wooden buildings. Justīne had lived here all her life—though it was not as if there was anywhere else to go. She knew The Old Town like the breath in her lungs: from her Dādi's house near the tree line, through the cobblestone streets where so many workshops and homes were clustered around the old cathedral; the guardhouse to the east, where apprentices honed their blades; to the bakery in the west, which made the breeze smell like bread; to the pockmarked woods to the north.

Throughout the day, the town was alight with activity, people working to fill the cellars and granaries, repairing rotting walls and metal tools, tending to the animals and—in Justīne's case—the fields. But at this hour, most were breaking for their midday meal and prayer, for repukdau. It created an eerie quiet as everyone returned to either their homes or the cathedral, their tools stilled and carts stationary. In the distance, one of Lilija's cattle mooed. Its somber voice echoed off the hills.

Justīne stood up and looked out beyond the wall, just to prove to herself that the dark wasn't creeping toward them. A narrow stretch of grass surrounded the wall at its base, ending at the bank of a shallow river. A stone bridge crossed it, with copper-lined railings that had turned a sickly blue-green color. It looked like it was ready to fall apart at any second. Not that it mattered, though. The bridge led into a dark cloud, a whirling mass of inky shadows, endlessly shifting—the maalkonis. Wispy particles floated inside of it, like dust in the wind, glimmering an unnatural violet in the midday light. If Justīne ignored all the corpses that must be inside of it, just out of sight, the dark was almost beautiful. In a strange and twisted kind of way.

"Do you see anything?" Anna asked, now at her side. She'd gotten quicker about the climb lately, more used to the footholds.

"No," Justīne said. "I don't think there's anything out there."

"What about the lost people?"

The *lost* were what they called those who fell to the maalkonis. They were people—Ļaodil and those who lived in other towns before the dark took them—who ventured into it or were overcome. They never came back. The adults considered them dead. If one of the Ļaodil was taken, they'd hold a ceremonial funeral, burning some of their possessions on the pyre, usually personal effects that others didn't need.

Everything else was given out to the Ļaodil, to whoever needed it most: food, tools, clothing, and so on. Dead or not, the lost were most certainly gone. As terrible as it was, nothing could be left to waste. Although she and Anna liked to look for the lost, in case somebody needed their help getting back, Justīne was struggling to believe that anything could survive out there. She had seen people become overwhelmed by and collapse in the maalkonis before, screaming like they'd been set aflame. Then, a few seconds later, silence.

Justīne still dreamed of Monika's last moments. The mage—the town's last mage—had long studied the maalkonis and attempted to push it away, even just temporarily. That afternoon, she'd walked out to the rusty copper bridge and, while she was still drawing her runes, the maalkonis surged forward. That had only been five years ago, when Justīne was ten years old and Anna eight. Moments before she was taken, their Dādi had been telling them about the things beyond The Old Town that he hoped Monika would help them see for the first time: vast pools of salt water, dense forests, and hills so tall that it could take *days* to scale them. Things they'd heard of before, stories passed down for generations from those who lived before the darkness spread.

After Monika was lost—or perhaps after she died—he didn't talk about those things much anymore.

Justīne asked her sister, "Do you think the stuff that Dādi used to talk about is still out there? The mountains, the salt water, and all the other towns where people used to live?"

Anna shrugged. "I'd like to see a real forest one day. Dādi told me that there used to be a dense one beyond the west wall, with far more trees than the logging fields in the hills." She paused, her gaze falling to the atstrumeter beside them. She stared closely at the machine's spinning gears and picked at the corrosion beginning to turn the copper the same blue-green color as the bridge. "Sometimes I wonder if we're the last people. You know? Maybe the maalkonis isn't a ring around us like the Lord Mayor says. What if it is *everything* around us? The Ḷaodil invented atstrumeters. We may be the only people who have them."

"I don't know. People used to trade before we were all cut off from each other. Maybe we were able to share a few, or the designs for them, before that happened." Justīne frowned at the darkness, her eyes following a cluster of violet wisps.

Anna frowned. "There's something out there," she said confidently. "I don't know what it is, or if it's even human, but I'd like to help find it. Even if it's just some plants that have found a way to live out in the dark. How wild would that be?"

A moment of silence passed between them, broken only by the several spinning atstrumeters. Then Anna added, "Dādi says he's going to apprentice me. Show me how he builds these machines."

Justīne pursed her lips. She had gotten to choose to work with Graudiņš, though it hadn't felt like much of a choice. While the old man had taken on help seasonally, he had no apprentice, and *somebody* had to learn to run the farm. Dādi had been insistent that it should be her.

She liked the farm, even if Graudiņš was grumpy and his cat hated her. She'd come to enjoy the feeling of dirt between her fingers and watching the plants grow each season.

"Are you looking forward to it?" she asked.

"I think so," Anna said. "Everyone looks to Dādi to keep us safe, but he keeps complaining about how the atstrumeters are wearing out. I'd like to help repair them and maybe make some better ones. Some quieter ones, at least."

"I can't imagine what it'd be like to not hear them buzzing constantly."

"Either way, I think it could be fun. Especially tinkering the way Dādi does, testing out new machines… And I could still study Monika's old books in my free time."

"Really? You think you can learn the runes without her?"

Anna shrugged. "Maybe. Not easily, but maybe. I've been reading her books while you've been working on the farm." Anna kicked a loose stone. It toppled over the edge and onto the long grass at the base of the wall. "I've learned a few things but they're so confusing. Monika wrote in them, which should have helped, but it's *impossible* to read her handwriting. And parts of the book look like even Monika wasn't sure how to use some of the runes. There are questions she wrote but never answered."

"Just be careful. Draw the wrong rune, and your hand could go"—Justīne flicked her fingers, miming an explosion—"*boom.*"

"Oh, I don't draw any," Anna said quickly. "I'd love to, but right now I'm just trying to understand how they work. What they mean. For now, anyway. It's like a whole other language."

The Old Town could have used a new mage. Magic was complicated and filled with rules that Justīne didn't understand, but to hear Dādi speak of Monika, she'd always found a way to help people, often in small ways like felling trees or helping the forge's fires burn stronger. But Justīne knew that her sister was right. Perhaps it was better that Anna was interested in engineering. Magic was powerful but unpredictable, even in the best of situations. At least they knew that the atstrumeters worked.

Justīne had overheard the Lord Mayor speaking with other adults about the need for more engineers. Dādi was the last one. He had been working longer days and had left at odd hours of the night, his fingers slick with black oil and grease by the time he returned. The problem was that they also needed more farmers, shepherds, smiths, cobblers, surgeons, and everything else. The Old Town was surviving, but only just.

"Come on," Justīne said and continued along the walkway. She would need to return to help Graudiņš with the farm soon, and all they'd done was fret about their futures.

"Where to?" Anna asked, following her.

"To see the nest."

"Oh, right!" Anna squealed and rushed past her.

"Hey!" Justīne stumbled and fell into the wall's railing. A brick rammed into her side, and she held in the jolt of pain through gritted teeth—not for fear of anything in the maalkonis, but because she didn't want any of the adults to spot them. The guard was always spread thin, and what patrol existed was out of sight for now, but so far away that they wouldn't hear her shout.

"Are you okay?" Anna asked. At some point she'd stopped and was watching her.

Justīne lifted her tunic and touched at her side where she'd landed against the rail. It stung, pain threading across her skin. There was no blood, but she was sure that it would be bruised come first dim.

"Be careful, Anna," Justīne said.

"I'm sorry." She pouted.

"If Dādi or the guards catch us up here—"

"I said I'm sorry. I really am," she whispered.

Justīne glanced back toward The Old Town, to a tall cathedral whose bell tower and two spires nearly reached the ever-present haze above. A thin grey mist spread from the maalkonis over them and obscured—but didn't fully block—the sun. Those towers also helped to hide them from the guard when they patrolled the other side of town. Surely Ešlija would be coming their way soon, though…

Ešlija often took the midday watch while most others broke for repukdau—the midday meal and prayer. Justīne also suspected that the guard had taken a liking to their Dādi. It remained to be seen if she would rat them out to get his approval, or if she'd keep their secrets to gain her and Anna's favor. Justīne hoped it was the latter, but she didn't want to test that theory if they didn't have to.

Justīne forced herself up and said, "Let's go. Hurry."

Justīne's side ached as she followed her sister along the walkway. They stopped beside a small cluster of trees in the southeast corner of town. The largest was an oak which bore branches that reached out into the maalkonis. Its boughs on the far side had splintered and their bark had been blackened as if they'd been burned. What few leaves remained gave off a violet sheen and grew in unusual shapes as if the maalkonis had warped the few which lived on the edge. The other half of the tree, the part facing them, was lush and green from the springtime rains.

Anna shot her a mischievous smile and then jumped over the wall. A heartbeat later, the nearest tree shook, and its leaves rustled against the others. Justīne looked down from the spot where she'd jumped. Anna was balancing on an elm's bough. It bent slightly under her weight as she leaned against its trunk. She glanced back up at Justīne and said, "Come on."

Justīne walked a few paces along the wall, across from another tree. An atstrumeter spun beside her, fastened to the bricks and rattling in its mount. She put a hand on the wall, trying to decide how to get through without kicking it off. One broken atstru wouldn't cause the maalkonis to crash down around them, but two or three might cause a leak they couldn't stop. It was a funny thing to know that these little copper spinners were all that held back certain death for them. And, if Anna was right, all of humanity.

A chill ran down Justīne's spine at the thought.

She climbed up on the railing. A brick shifted underfoot. Justīne steadied herself, took a breath, and leapt onto the bough of an old pine tree. She braced herself against the tree as she landed. She could immediately feel the sap on her arm. She tried to wipe it off on her trousers, which she immediately regretted.

"Oof." Anna grimaced at her from the elm.

"You could have moved aside," Justīne grumbled.

"You didn't ask."

Justīne rolled her eyes at her sister. They both made their way down. Anna descended the elm like a squirrel, moving as if this were as natural as walking or breathing. Justīne followed with far less grace, eager to get out of the sticky pine as quickly as possible.

Once they were both on the narrow strip of ground between the maalkonis and the wall, Anna inched toward the giant, half-destroyed oak. They stood no more than a few paces away from the roiling darkness.

"Careful," Justīne said, mostly out of habit. The maalkonis was known to shift and lunge forward at times, but that was rare, especially during the day. Something about the light helped to hold it back.

"I know," she whispered back like a reflex. "Come here. Look at this."

Among the lowest and strongest boughs of the half-destroyed oak lay a small nest made of grass, twigs, and rusty orange fur from Graudiņš' cat—the only creature in the old town to have such a distinctive coat. In the center rested three robin eggs, each white with reddish-brown speckles. However, one egg was different. Buried partially beneath a damaged piece of the nest, it was darker, larger, and its speckles were shades of blue and red. That one was their favorite. Anna liked the colors. Justīne was just curious why one egg was so different and was eager to see it hatch. When Justīne leaned in closer, she noticed that the strange egg had cracked.

"It's hatching!" Anna said and waited for the egg to shake as the chick tried to pull itself free of the shell. Instead, the seconds dragged on, and the egg didn't so much as twitch. "Oh no," Anna whispered, holding a hand to her mouth.

"Maybe it needs more time?" Justīne offered, uncertain how long it took a bird to hatch from an egg. She knew that Lilija's chickens hatched from eggs, but she'd only been around to see it happen once or twice. Still, a sinking feeling nestled deep in her stomach.

"It's not moving, June. Do you think it needs help? We can bring the nest to Lilija. She would know what to do."

"I doubt she'd want to. Even if she does, wouldn't the birds' mother have trouble finding them later? She might abandon the whole nest if she thinks we tampered with her eggs."

Anna shrugged. "But it might be stuck or hurt, and the maalkonis…"

She shrugged back at her sister. "They'll be flying off long before the Maalkonis reaches them. Besides, Lilija is busy, and we don't know the first thing about raising birds."

"I bet we could figure it out."

The cracked egg was still as the grave. She decided not to suggest that it might have already passed, partly for Anna, partly because Justīne didn't want to say it.

"You gonna' go digging for worms to feed them? And you can't show them how to be birds so they'd be dependent on you. Might not even learn to fly."

"I figured birds could figure that out on their own."

"Maybe. I'd bet seeing their mama fly around helps, though." Justīne glanced down at Anna's legs. "I bet they'd get real good at running around watching you. Graudiņš' cat would love that."

"Pūka would never." Anna huffed. A heartbeat later she put her hands up in surrender. "Okay, she absolutely would. Fine. I won't save the little birds from the evil dark magic cloud literally two paces away from them."

"Two *human* paces. Probably three dozen *robin* paces." Anna laughed.

"Actually, the birds' mama chose a great spot. They're right next to an atstru," Justīne said, gesturing up at the one she'd stepped over along the wall. As she did, she caught sight of a figure peering through the trees.

"Anna? Justīne?" a woman's voice asked, incredulous. Ešlija.

"Hells," Anna whispered.

Justīne stood frozen in place. If they were really quiet, maybe Ešlija would think she was hearing things and move along. If she did, all they had to do was climb back up, then let her catch them somewhere else, and pretend they'd been *there* all afternoon. It would take some convincing, but it wasn't completely impossible. Justīne could sprint back to the farm and stay there until Ešlija's patrol crossed her path again. Graudiņ was taking repukdau, so Ešlija couldn't prove that they *hadn't* been at the farm all midday.

"I can see both of you," Ešlija interrupted Justīne's thoughts, peering at them through the trees. Her tone hardened as she commanded them, "Get up here. Now."

"Hells," Justīne cursed.

Nearby, a robin's chirp caught their attention. It was perched on the pine Justīne had used to catch her fall, watching them intently. Its red face and breast stood out against the shadows and the maalkonis behind it. It began to make a racket, fluttering up and down the branch, its call a shrill, high-pitched threat.

"Sorry," Justīne told the bird. Then to Anna, "Let's go."

They clambered up the elm tree. Justīne's hands, still sticky with sap, came away with dirt and bark under her fingernails as she let Ešlija help her back onto the wall. She wiped off what she could while the guard pulled Anna back up as well.

With both of them back over the ledge, Ešlija put her hands on her hips, reminding Justīne of how Dādi looked when he was upset. She was probably a few years younger than him. Dādi's hair had recently taken on streaks of grey, whereas Ešlija's was still dark brown all the way down to her hips—though at the moment, she'd fastened it into a large bun. She also wore a faded yellow cloak over a layer of chainmail. A short sword hung off her belt; an arquebus and powder horn hung off a strap she'd slung over her shoulder.

"What the hells were you thinking, going over the wall like that?" she demanded. "You shouldn't be up on the wall at all, let alone *outside* of it. One wrong step, and there's nothing any of us can do to help you. At best, you end up like Bruno and lose a few fingers. At worst... You both understand that, right?"

Anna nodded. She was staring down at her feet.

"There's a robin's nest beyond the wall, down there." Justīne nodded toward the place they'd just been. With them back on the wall, the bird's frantic chirping had quieted. Justīne hoped that it was on the nest, helping warm and protect the remaining eggs. "We discovered it last week."

"You've been sneaking out for a week?" Ešlija asked the question as if there was no air in her lungs.

Justīne grimaced. She hadn't meant to reveal that.

"Not every day," Anna said, no doubt trying to make it better.

"How did you slip out with nobody noticing?"

Justīne glanced at her sister. After she shrugged back at her, Justīne decided that they probably didn't have anything left to hide. After all, Ešlija had already caught them.

"There are only twenty people on the guard," she said, "but well more than half of you have other duties to attend to. Teodor helps his dādi at the butchery, Ievan mostly works the forge, and so on. The Lord Mayor's guard—people like Niklāvs—mostly just stands around him… Besides that, the rest of you spend time training your apprentices, and everybody needs to sleep or eat at some point. The night shift rests during the day, and midday is when most of you work your other jobs or break for repukdau. Which is fair; you need to eat and say your prayers as well. But at most, that leaves only one or two guards around this time of day. If that person's on the north wall, trees block their vision, and in other parts you can't see through the old cathedral. So when you're walking past the farm, you can't hope to see this part of the town.

"You also tend to walk in groups, rather than covering all angles, so there's always a decent amount of time when any given part of the wall is out of sight, assuming the person or people on watch keep moving. Sometimes you stop to talk with somebody in town, or whoever relieves you of your shift. That's plenty of time to explore the places where the maalkonis doesn't quite reach the wall. And the wall is so old that pieces of it have chipped away, so it's easy to climb once you find the right place."

Ešlija took a deep breath and pinched the bridge of her nose. The long sigh that escaped her lips was more ominous than the darkness that surrounded their town. Justīne worried that she'd given away too much. Perhaps she'd only worsened things for them. Anna wasn't helping. She looked a little *too* proud at having outsmarted the adults. Justīne was as well, she had to admit, but she didn't want Ešlija to know that. She nudged Anna in the arm, and her devilish grin became a little snarl. A bit dramatic, but at least she didn't look so happy about tricking the guard anymore.

"You're right." Ešlija chuckled without a hint of mirth. "We have been lax lately. The maalkonis hasn't shifted much in the past few years. Not that we could *fight* it, but we still must be vigilant and keep track of it. But vigilance too easily becomes routine. Things are going to have to change. We can't have children running around outside the walls."

"We weren't running," Anna said. Justīne thought back to when her sister had sped past her, knocking her into the wall just minutes ago, but chose not to mention that.

Ešlija glanced up at them.

"What will you change?" Anna asked more cautiously.

"Well, for starters I think we'll take your sister's advice. Two guards at all times, minimum, on opposing sides of the wall. That way we can see most angles and make sure nothing gets in or *out*."

"Makes sense." Justīne nodded. She just hoped they weren't in trouble.

Ešlija watched her for a moment. Then, "I know you're busy with your apprenticeship, Justīne, but clearly you have some time to yourself. Both of you. You should visit me sometime at the guardhouse. I'd be happy to mentor you too, Anna. We need smart kids like you keeping watch, capable of fighting whatever crawls out of the maalkonis. Not that anything has yet, but we really don't know what lurks out there or what it might be capable of."

"I'm going to be an engineer," Anna said.

"And Dādi already showed us how to use a sword," Justīne added.

Ešlija grinned, her face turning a slight shade of red. "Your Dādi means well, but he's an engineer. Doesn't really know a thing about fencing."

"All you do is swing it around," Anna said, as if Ešlija had never thought of such a thing.

"Yes," Ešlija said, "but sometimes there's something on the other end, trying to swing back at you!" Ešlija lunged forward, catching Anna by surprise. Anna laughed and stepped back, taking up her best impression of a fighter's stance.

"What does it really matter?" Justīne asked. "Nothing ever comes out of the maalkonis."

"We don't know for sure that nothing ever *will*," Ešlija said. "Didn't you just scold *me* about being too relaxed? Besides, not all threats lie outside these walls."

Justīne didn't like what she was suggesting, but Dādi had told them about how, before the maalkonis had encircled the walls, people fought over everything from food to land, or bragging rights. It sounded barbaric, but clearly Ešlija was worried that could happen again. The thought hadn't even crossed Justīne's mind. To her, it seemed like the Ļaodil all helped each other, no matter what they were going through. It was hard to imagine anything else.

Ešlija said, "You two train with me every now and then, and maybe I won't tell your Dādi about what you were up to here."

Anna gasped. "Does that mean we can come back to see the robin's—"

"*No*," Ešlija interrupted. "If I so much as catch a glimpse of the two of you on the wall again—Gods forbid if you leave town—I will personally see to it that you two have latrine duty for the rest of the year."

Justīne physically recoiled. She was used to spreading fertilizer on the farm. She'd grown especially used to it over the last week. But the latrines were a different sort of torture. "It's *spring*," she said.

Ešlija nodded. "Sure is. If you won't consider your own safety—or each other's—then think about what living horror cleaning those out in the middle of summer would be."

"Stop, stop," Anna shouted. Then softly, "We won't leave again."

"We promise," Justīne added quickly.

The silence that followed was long, filled only by the whirring of the atstrumeters around them.

"Good," Ešlija said finally. "Get out of here, then. While I'm still in a good mood. And I expect you to see me in the ring soon. Be ready to pick up a sword. You'll need to work hard to unlearn whatever drivel your dādi has taught you about fighting." She spat off the edge of the wall. When Ešlija looked back at them, there was a breezy smile on her lips. "Don't worry. It'll be fun!"

Justīne spent the rest of the day helping at Graudiņš' farm. She watered the spring barley and then set about preparing another patch of soil for planting the new crop. She borrowed one of Lilija's bulls, who helped her turn over the soil for the season. It wasn't exciting work. The bull did most of the heavy lifting, but she needed to keep the plow upright and steer it—and occasionally she'd need to stop to move a rock or let the bull rest.

Lilija had been adamant about taking care of the bull, practically threatening her and Graudiņš should he hurt himself. It seemed a bit much, but Justīne had come to expect that sort of thing from the shepherd. It would have been weird if she hadn't complained or antagonized them over it, but even she understood the importance of a good harvest. At least the bull, Uli, was pleasant to be around.

Justīne kept the plow steady, carving neat rows in the soil. The air smelled raw and musty—both from the turned earth and when the wind shifted. Graudiņš was fertilizing the plants in the greenhouse.

Ešlija's words, and her threat of latrine duty, weighed on Justīne's mind. Had she been joking? She didn't think the guard was dishonest, but anyone else would have dragged her and Anna to Dādi after catching them over the wall. Why *had* she decided to keep it a secret?

Maybe she was overthinking it, Justīne decided, as sweat formed along her brow and rolled down her neck. The Ļaodil had always done their best to protect each other. Especially the children—and Justīne knew that many of them still viewed her as such. Despite the fact that she worked nearly every day from first to last dim. Which was completely unfair, considering she *also* worked as much as they did. If not more. However, it also wasn't an argument she could win yet. So, perhaps this was Ešlija's way of protecting them.

Regardless, she and Anna would have to be careful. If Dādi began asking the right questions, Justīne had no doubt that Ešlija's resolve would crack. It was obvious in the way that she found reasons to stop by the house, the way her voice changed when they spoke, that she was in love with him. Was *love* the right word? Either way, it was a wonder how Dādi didn't seem to notice.

Justīne couldn't remember her mother. She'd gotten sick when Anna was only two years old, and Justīne had been four. She didn't love the idea of Ešlija taking her place, but she did like the woman. There was nothing exactly *wrong* with her, and it was hard to replace somebody Justīne never really knew. If she and Dādi decided to be together, she wouldn't try to get in the way of it.

The plow skipped over a rock, sending a shock up her arms, but it kept moving. The bull didn't seem to notice. It plodded along, maintaining a good pace. Justīne called up to him, "I couldn't do this without you, Uli. And the old man *really* wants the plowing done today, so thank you."

The bull snorted.

"I mean it," she said. "Remind me to get you a treat after this. Maybe a few—you'll have more than earned it. Just don't tell Lilija. She'll think I *spoiled your diet* or something." Justīne scoffed.

She paused as Graudiņš emerged from the greenhouse. The old man hunched forward, and his muscles sagged off of his bones. A thin white beard framed his chin, and his hair was cut short, revealing a wide bald spot. Pūka, his cat, followed a few paces behind.

"There you are, girl," Graudiņš said. Then he sniffed the air dramatically. "Seems like that bull's been helping you spread fertilizer."

"He's a team player," she said, not slowing down. "Just watch where you step."

Graudiņš walked beside her. However, the cat found a butterfly to chase, its wings the color of ash. It flitted around the farmhouse, and Pūka prowled after it.

Graudiņš watched her chase it, a smile on his thin lips. "There she goes. You'd think after so many years I'd get sick of spring. And I do always dread its coming, but then I miss it when the season's gone. The plowing, the warmth after a long winter, that sweet smell of earth and shit… The work is like a sweaty prayer for a good harvest." He made a gesture with his hand, folding it over his heart, and added, "Gods willing."

Justīne wiped sweat off her brow. It came away in a sheet along her arm. "I wish that it were a windier day, so that the *sweet* smell from your greenhouse might be carried away faster."

Graudiņš laughed, his belly shaking. "You're quick-witted, girl. You must get that from your mother. Oļegs only thinks of the little copper instruments he tinkers with. Bah."

"You know the atstrumeters are what keep the maalkonis at bay," she jabbed back at her mentor. She shouldn't talk back, but it was insensitive of him to talk about her Dādi that way.

He shrugged. "Without a good harvest, none of those copper trinkets matter. One bad season, and this whole town starves. And once that happens, things get ugly real quick. Trust me. So, I hope you say your prayers at each mealtime. The Gods are petty bastards, and we can't afford their ire, 'specially not Thirst's. That one's only trouble, I don't care what anyone says. But don't tell them I said that. Keep at it, girl. There is much to do. The sooner we prepare these fields, the sooner we can plant them, and the better we'll be ready come winter."

"And where will you be, Graudiņš?" Justīne asked the sacrilegious coot. She could hear the sharp tone in her voice and quickly added, "Just in case I need to find you later."

"Only one plow, only one bull." Graudiņš continued in a quieter voice, "I do appreciate you taking over for me this year, Justīne. My knees don't work so good no more."

"Of course," Justīne said.

"We do need this done today, though. I'll lend you a hand. Don't you worry, I'll grab the hoe and till the smaller gardens for a bit, do what I can before the legs give out. Then I'll get back to the greenhouse. More to do there, and I can sit for most of it."

"I'm only about a halfway through, though. I don't want to kill Uli over this. Lilija would have my head. Yours too."

Graudiņš scowled and looked up at the cloudy sky. "I hoped you'd be further along. There's a storm coming, and I want to get as much ready before it rains. This is a good omen, but as usual, it's damned poor timing. We'll have to do the greenhouse tomorrow. And I'll see if I can steal somebody else to help you out before it starts storming."

"How do you know it's going to rain?"

"Old folk always know." He winked then succumbed to a fit of coughing. After he caught his breath, he added, "There's a shift in the air. Even through the maalkonis, you can *feel* it get heavy with moisture, like a weight in the bones. It is not a heavy storm, but it'll be here soon. I'll be back. You keep that bull moving."

The old man sounded mad, but she wasn't going to say it. Graudiņš was usually right about these things. Maybe Justīne just wasn't old enough to feel whatever he was talking about. Or the sweat that blanketed her skin made it too hard to notice. Either way, she did as he asked and kept Uli moving, carving fresh gouges into the fields.

The sky darkened, then rain began to trickle down through the thin layer of the maalkonis overhead. It was light at first, almost impossible to notice. Justīne's clothes stuck to her skin, and sweat stung her eyes. The rain slowly washed it away and replaced sweat with water.

Graudiņš had found help in town. The butcher's son, Teodor, and the surgeon, Sofija, came to help. Armed with an assortment of hand plows and hoes, they worked through a few of the smaller plots. They moved much slower than Uli, but any little bit helped. The bull had begun to slow down, and they still had about a quarter of the fields to go. Justīne urged him on, promising rest and treats once they were done. She couldn't imagine how tired he was. All she was doing was keeping the plow from going off course, and she was exhausted. Her back and arms screamed as they turned around, carving yet another furrow.

In the distance, she could hear Graudiņš barking orders as he worked. Once, when he sent Sofija to check on her, she told the surgeon to send the old man inside. The rain pounded against them, a haze of white in the air, and Justīne worried that he would fall ill. Sofija agreed and said she would try again. The old fool didn't leave the field until she and Uli had finished.

Justīne paid her debt to Uli, sneaking into the farmhouse cellar to grab a few melon rinds for the bull and dried apricot slices for herself. The heist was easy with the old man already fast asleep. She enjoyed her snack with Uli, out behind the farmhouse. The dried apricots made her crave the fresh ones when they would be ripe for picking this summer. Uli nudged the hand she held them with, and she laughed.

"I can't give you any, they're no good for bulls, even strong ones like you. I don't want to get you sick," Justīne said, and put another rind in his mouth. The bull's tongue wrapped around it, and his giant molars crunched down loudly. "That's better, huh?"

She let the bull rest for a bit longer then walked Uli to Lilija's barn. When Justīne finally got home, the rain had slowed down a bit. She wrung out her clothes at the door as much as she could then changed into an old tunic and trousers. They were slightly small and torn at the hem, but at least they were dry.

Dādi had already gotten a small fire started. It sputtered and sang in the hearth, thin grey smoke swirling up the chimney. Its warmth wrapped around Justīne like a gentle hug. She hung her wet clothes on a line beside it. Water dripped off them and onto the floor.

Dādi sat at his workbench near the fire. He wore a plain tunic and trousers, both as stained with oil and grease as his hands were. He was tinkering with some new copper device. It looked similar to the atstrumeters along the wall but with a trigger mechanism, and more of the cogs were exposed to the air. Or perhaps he just hadn't gotten around to building the casing yet. Anna sat beside him on a stool, watching attentively.

"June," Dādi said, his voice unconcerned but firm. He pushed his spectacles up the bridge of his nose, keeping his attention on his work. "Move the rushes out of the way. If they get wet, they could become moldy. You know better."

Justīne kicked the dried grass mat away from where she'd hung her clothes up. It skid along the floor and spun up the odor of the herbs strewn into the mat.

"I saw that Graudiņš was out in that storm with you," Dādi continued, still focused on his work. "He shouldn't be out in the rain. He's a tough brute, but he's still an old man. If he catches ill…"

"I told Sofija to make him go inside. *He* didn't listen," Justīne said.

She dragged the bench closer to the fire. When it was near enough, she set it down and lay across it on her back. She stretched and ran her hands through her long brown hair, her fingers catching and breaking through where it was knotted. She needed to brush it, but her comb was all the way in her and Anna's bedroom.

She looked over at where Anna sat with Dādi. He stared back at her. "I'm sorry," she sighed. "It was selfish of me to accept Graudiņš' help in the first place, especially when he told me there was a storm coming."

Dādi set down his tools. "June, you are not selfish. One cannot coax an ox into being quiet at prayer. But it doesn't mean you shouldn't at least try."

"What's that?"

"What?"

"An *ox*."

Dādi sucked his lips before answering, his eyes glazing over for a moment. Then he said, "Oxen were like big cows, but with wide horns. They were used for carrying and pulling heavy things. We used to have a few here when I was about your age, but… Not anymore."

"How big were their horns?" Anna asked, sitting up a bit.

Dādi spread his arms a comically wide distance.

"You're lying." Justīne laughed.

"I would never!" Dādi said, aghast. "They were usually gentle creatures, like those bulls Lilija has, but you still had to watch yourself around them, or they could accidentally give you a good stabbing."

Anna giggled. "You used to live with such monsters?"

"Not monsters, *meita*. Animals. Companions. Like the goats, cows, and chickens that Lilija looks after. They can be a little scary sometimes, but so is your big sister."

"Hey!" Justīne said, extending a hand toward him like a claw.

Dādi held Anna back and feigned terror. Then Anna giggled, and his façade broke.

A knock came at the door, and Ešlija stepped inside, a copper torch in her hand. It was an odd-looking device, a torch with no flame. The wooden shaft was topped with a copper mechanism that held a wire in the center, which was surrounded by a crown of wrought iron, like the guard of a sword. Dādi had explained how it worked to Justīne a few times, how the sun's energy powered it during the day so that it could burn at night, but it still seemed as arcane as magic to her.

"Greetings, Oļegs," Ešlija said, shouldering the torch. "I'm headed to the ring with Gustavs. You girls still want to come with me?"

"Now?" Anna asked.

Dādi looked up at her questioningly.

"Yes," she told Anna. Then to Dādi, "I ran into Justīne and Anna today. They… They expressed interest in learning the sword."

"That's right," Justīne said, sitting up on the bench. "We thought it might be fun to train with Ešlija."

Anna frowned. "Dādi was showing me how these panels connect… And then after that I was going to go read—"

"I can show you that more later," Dādi interrupted her. "If Ešlija has time for you now, you should join her. You couldn't pick a better teacher. She makes even the *maalkonis* quake in fear."

"Stop," Ešlija told him. Justīne narrowed her eyes at her. Was their 'fearsome' guard blushing, or was that a trick of the light?

"I'd like to work on this a bit more"—Dādi gestured at the device—"and I will need more time yet to prepare *vekrēla* afterward. So, take your time."

"Oh, if you need their help to cook, I can come back at a better time."

Dādi shrugged. "It's quicker if they do, but better that they practice with you. My work makes it difficult to find the time to show them how to wield a blade. Plus, I only have the one sword. Makes practices pretty dull.

June, why don't you get my blade from that chest there. The edges are already blunted, and it should be light enough that it'll work for Anna as well."

Justīne unlatched and opened the chest he indicated. Below some unfolded clothes was an old sword, the edges too dull to cut, the iron showing patches of rust. She hadn't picked it up since starting her apprenticeship with Graudiņš, but it felt comfortable enough in her hands.

"That's the one," Dādi said.

Ešlija groaned. "You need to let me clean that thing up later."

"It's clean enough."

"It's *rusting*. I'm tempted to have Ievan melt it down and have the forge salvage it into something more useful. That boy doesn't get much iron to work with. I'm sure he'd be thrilled."

Dādi pointed his unfinished copper device at her. "If you hand Ievan my sword, I'll have him start melting down your shit too. Could start with some of that armor you're wearing. It's so old, after all."

"Oh, you want to take a shot at my mail?" Ešlija stepped forward then relented, smiling at him. "Fine. I'll see if I can polish that rusty old blade for you tomorrow. For today, it'll be *fine* I suppose."

"If you're going to repair that, you and your boy should stay for vekrēla after you're all done at the ring. Please. It's the least I can do."

Ešlija looked like she was about to refuse, but then her expression changed. "What are you planning to make?"

"Not sure yet. But I've got some smoked pork from Krišs' that I need to use. A few dried apricots still around that I could toss into something… I'll figure the rest out later. Depends a bit on how much longer I'm fussing over this trinket. Either way, I don't think you'll want to miss it," he added with a wink.

"Alright." Ešlija laughed. "Deal."

❧

As they arrived at the training yard, the sun's rays eked through the dark. A weak haze of gold and orange hung above the dark shadows coming from the wall, the maalkonis behind it glittering faint purple sparks in the dying light. Ešlija's son was already there, whacking a blunted sword against a training dummy. With each strike, dried grass burst through the ratty old clothes it had been stuffed into.

"Gustavs," Ešlija called to him.

"Yeah." The boy stopped and stepped forward, wiping a hand along his brow that glistened with either sweat or rain. Gustavs was older than Justīne, but only by about ten months. Despite that, he stood nearly a head taller than her. She stood a little straighter as Gustavs approached them.

"Oļegs' kids are interested in training with us," Ešlija said. "Isn't that right, you two?"

Justīne nodded.

"I love fighting," Anna said, raising her hands like the claws of some monster. She was smiling, but a faint growl escaped her lips.

Justīne rolled her eyes.

"That right?" Gustavs laughed.

Ešlija said, "I don't think I've ever seen you girls spar. Justīne, why don't we start with you? We'll see what you need to work on and go from there. Gustavs promises he'll go easy on you." She gave her son a stern look and told him, "Keep your blade below the neck."

He rolled his eyes. "When have I ever—"

"Yesterday."

"Only because you knocked my blade up," he fired back.

Justīne looked between the guard and her apprentice. She thought she'd be sparring with the training dummy, not another person, let alone Ešlija's son. Though, this was a fairer fight, she supposed. She just didn't want to hurt Gustavs. Her Dādi's training sword, blunted though it was, could still leave a solid bruise. She was about to ask if they were certain, but the look on both of their faces showed no hint of humor. If anything, Gustavs seemed excited to fight the way he began stretching his arms and legs.

"Alright," Justīne said, and stepped into the ring with Gustavs.

The training ring was about ten meters wide, a low barrier of logs marking the edges. They were so old that half were rotting, sprouting white mushrooms and green moss, sinking into the ground. The well-trodden dirt inside had turned to mud after the rains. She dragged a boot over it, testing how slippery the ground was.

Gustavs took up a fighting stance, opposite her. He held his sword with one hand then turned his body sideways—making himself a smaller target. Justīne knew that Gustavs was more practiced than she was. He'd been Ešlija's apprentice for as long as Justīne could remember, but she'd assumed that somebody so close in age to her couldn't be *that* much better. Suddenly, this no longer felt like a fair fight. She watched him closely and gripped her sword tight.

"Whenever you're ready, farm girl," Gustavs said, giving his blade a slight flick as if he were beckoning her.

Justīne mimicked his stance: one hand on her Dādi's sword, the other back and out of the way. It felt awkward, so she stopped trying to tilt her body so much. Once she felt mostly comfortable, Justīne gave Gustavs a nod.

Gustavs lunged forward, his sword a blur in the dim light, but she was able to block his first strike. Their blades rang out. She felt the collision through her grip. She tried to push Gustavs back with a wide swing, but he was already swinging at her again, and she felt his blunted blade against her arm. His touch was noticeable but light. She realized that he wasn't just faster than her, but he also was controlling how much weight he put behind each swing—and he was holding back. Had he been trying, she was sure that would have hurt.

"Point, Gustavs," Ešlija said from behind her.

"Points?" Justīne asked, still a bit startled by how quickly it was over.

"In a real fight, there are few second chances. But here, we score how many times somebody makes contact. One point per time you strike your opponent, then you start over after the point's been awarded and go again. It's an old system from a game that we used to play in tournaments. Haven't held any in a while though. Anyway, ready up. Justīne, this time make sure to hold your sword up higher. Your guard is too low."

Gustavs took up his fighting stance again, and Justīne did the same then raised her elbows a little. Out of the corner of her eye, she saw somebody walking by: Staņislavs, the carpenter's apprentice, with his sister, Sofija. She waved at them as they passed.

"Focus," Gustavs said.

"I'll do the instruction, thank you," Ešlija said. "But he's right. Don't let yourself get distracted, Justīne."

Justīne adjusted her grip on the sword and refocused her attention on Gustavs. She took a breath, trying to calm her nerves. This time, she wouldn't let him get the first move. At the very least, she didn't want to lose as quickly this time. Especially if other people were watching.

Justīne lunged forward. She brought her Dādi's sword down on Gustavs, but he blocked it. Rather than simply push against her, he redirected her sword to the side. Before Justīne could recover, Gustavs made a quick swing, and his blunted blade grazed her stomach. It was already over. Again.

Behind her, Ešlija declared, "Point, Gustavs."

"I hope you're better with the barley," Gustavs whispered with a grin.

Justīne cut off whatever Ešlija was saying when she took up her position once more—two hands on her sword this time—and said, "Again."

She was tired and sore from her day finishing the plowing, from climbing up and down the wall, but she put all that aside for the time being. She was going to score a point on this prick, and she would make it *hurt*.

Gustavs glanced at her, his smile fading, and took up his own fighting stance once more.

Another clash of blades, but this time Justīne threw all of her weight into the blade. Gods take *control*; she would never have Gustavs' precision, but she might be able to surprise or overpower him. Gustavs stumbled as he attempted to step backward under her assault, catching his heel on one of the logs that marked the ring's boundary. Justīne swung her leg out to trip him, and Gustavs collapsed in the muddy ring. She struck his leg with her blade, landing a blow before he could recover. It made a satisfying, heavy *thud*.

"Good job, Justīne! Your point," Ešlija said, and Anna cheered. Then, "That looked like a solid hit. Are you alright, Gustavs?"

"Fine," he said, recentering himself in the ring.

Justīne couldn't help but notice the way he was favoring his other leg and smiled at him. If he noticed her slight, he ignored it.

"That was smart," he told her. "When you're in a fight, you need to adapt to the situation. I shouldn't have stumbled like that, but I did, and you took advantage."

Justīne nodded. It felt weird for the person she'd just knocked down and attacked to compliment her. All she managed was, "Thanks."

Over the next several bouts, Justīne scored only a few more points on Gustavs. Ešlija advised her after each one. She'd been telegraphing her movements too much, placing too much weight on her right foot, and lacked control over her sword. Ešlija kept repeating that she couldn't just throw all her strength into it, but it was awfully tempting.

Even so, she knew that Ešlija was right. Gustavs could—most of the time—predict exactly where she'd swing at him. It was infuriating, and Justīne was swinging so hard that her arms were beginning to burn. Gustavs was able to knock her blade aside and create an opening. She struggled to overcome the errors that Ešlija pointed out, but her body refused to listen.

"What's the point of this anyway?" Justīne asked after six straight losses. "Guards carry arquebuses. If anything threatened us, you'd just shoot it."

"That's true," Ešlija said. "But our black powder is limited to what we had before the maalkonis surrounded us. Our families stockpiled what they could, but after so many centuries, it has dwindled. Not to mention that what little we *do* have can be ruined if it gets wet. But you can sharpen or repair a sword and spear, both of which won't misfire in the rain. It's best that you get familiar with the weight of a blade in your hand. And hopefully you'll never need to use one."

Justīne nodded. It made sense. She'd never given their stock of black powder much thought. She wondered how old it was. Stories of the maalkonis told of how it arrived a thousand years ago, but it had taken time to spread. Dādi told them once about how *his* dādi used to be able to wander the edge of The Old Town and fish in the river or work in the forest. Nobody had seen the forest or any fish in ages, though.

She pushed those thoughts out of her mind. What mattered was the fight in front of her with Gustavs. As frustrating as he was, and as exhausted as Justīne felt—her brow was once again slick with sweat—Justīne noticed that she couldn't help but smile a little after each bout.

And when she scored a point on Gustavs, that was the *best* feeling. She was starting to understand why they spent so much time training in the ring.

They went a few more rounds, until Ešlija finally asked Anna take her place. She didn't score a single point against Gustavs, but she never gave up trying. Unfortunately, the sword seemed to be a bit too heavy in her hands, and her attempts to strike Gustavs were far too slow—despite the fact that Gustavs was moving much slower than he had in their bouts. Anna *had* gotten close to nicking him more than once. Justīne couldn't tell if he was taking it easy on Anna, or perhaps their earlier fights had tired Gustavs out more than she realized. Either way, Justīne watched him closely, hoping to learn how he moved. Next time, she wouldn't let him win so easily.

They left the ring at noctis, after the sun had set. The only light came from the glow from Ešlija's torch. The wire in its copper head burned a dim orange-gold and cast its light around The Old Town. Long shadows shifted behind the homes and trees that they passed, all moving in unison around them.

Anna was still talking sword fighting strategy with Ešlija, carrying Dādi's sword. Justīne was exhausted, but she listened to their conversation carefully. Ešlija was describing how to parry and block, reassuring Anna that if she kept practicing, her reaction time would improve.

They could smell food as they approached the house. Dādi was almost finished preparing vekrēla: rich broth and warm bread, sizzling meats and aromatic vegetables. It made Justīne's mouth water, and Ešlija swore at everything he'd made. After changing into fresh clothes, Justīne helped Dādi plate the food. Anna was nowhere to be seen.

Dādi shouted, "Anna, come set the table, please. Five plates."

She emerged from their room holding one of Monika's books, her lips moving wordlessly as she read from it. Justīne caught a glimpse of the text. The ink was partially faded, darker sketches of arcane runes on the edges of the pages. Some text was crossed out, replaced with a note written by the late mage.

Dādi was portioning stew into shallow bowls when he saw her. He put down the ladle and grabbed Anna by her shoulder, rushing her back into her room. Their conversation was quiet, but Justīne heard enough.

"We have company," Dādi said forcefully. His tone was not cruel, but it also was not to be questioned. Somehow, that made it scarier. And then she heard him say, "If you are going to start engineering, you cannot keep playing with these books."

Anna said something quietly.

Dādi said, "Yes, it is playing, because I have told you that you *cannot* draw any runes. It is too dangerous. Mages have a knack for getting themselves hurt, lost, or worse. So no more, okay?"

The rest of their brief conversation was too quiet for Justīne to hear. Ešlija had also come into the kitchen and asked where she could find plates and cups. When Justīne showed her, she and Gustavs set the table. When Dādi and Anna returned—without the book this time—all that was left was to bring the food to the table.

Justīne was stunned by how much there was. It reminded her of a midsummer feast. There was a dark rye loaf, still steaming, which Dādi had fetched from the Mayor Lord's wife, Beatrice. Two bowls of bacon- and onion-filled pīrāgi sat at either end of the table. In the center lay a large pot of stew made with pork, peas, onion, carrots, and apricot. Little was fresh, but this time of year they were used to dried and stale food. Cooking it as Dādi had made it difficult to tell, though.

Dādi took the hands of those sitting nearest to him—Anna and Ešlija—and the rest of the table did the same. He led the vekrēla prayer. "Blessed are the Gods who give us this meal as well as the means with which to make it. Thanks be to Thirst, with whom we share this food and drink."

"By your Light," the table responded in unison. Among their chorus, Anna was notably pouting. Justīne did as the others and ignored her.

It was a bit late for the prayer, and Justīne wanted nothing to do with it as her stomach churned for the delicious food spread out in front of her, but she played her part all the same. Graudiņš' warning of petty Gods rang in her head. Better to play it safe.

"Blessed is the Lord who breathes life into this world and the next, who gifted us with not only Souls, but also this Garden to call home. Would that the spirits and the departed could know our gratitude."

"By your Light."

"Blessed is Sun who shelters us in their Light, who keeps us and our town safe from the dark. Who delivered the gift of copper and steel. Would that the spirits and departed may share your protection."

"By your Light."

Dādi glanced up at the table. "Now, somebody tell me how Justīne ended up with all the damned pīrāgi around *her* chair?"

Justīne shot him a smile while she took two for herself—and only *then* passed the bowl to Dādi.

For a time, the room was quiet as everyone dug into the meal. Everything was incredible. It even seemed to break Anna out of her sulky mood. Dādi liked to cook, but it wasn't often that he did so much all at once. Not to mention the effort that went into filling and folding all of the pīrāgi. They weren't as fresh as the ones at last midsummer, and they were filled with far more onion than bacon, but they were still incredible. Even the bread coating had a satisfying crunch. After she had a few, Justīne scooped stew from her bowl with a slice of rye, savoring the meat and the bits of sweetness mixed in from the fruit.

"You've outdone yourself, Oļegs," Ešlija said, having just put aside her own stew to try one of the pīrāgi. She stared into the pocket of filling as if something inside might reveal secrets to her. "I'm not complaining, but I hope you didn't go through all this trouble on our behalf."

He shrugged. "I hadn't made a big meal in a while. You and Gustavs coming gave me the excuse I needed."

Justīne resisted the urge to ask Ešlija to marry her Dādi, so that they could eat like this every day.

"But," he continued, "I haven't heard about how the kids did at the ring."

Ešlija straightened her back and swallowed the bite she'd been chewing. "They both did well, especially considering Gustavs' been training with me since he was no older than five years. Justīne even scored a few points on him."

"I let her score those points," Gustavs said quickly, gesturing at her with his fork.

"You did *not*," Justīne spat back at him.

"I would hope not," Ešlija said, eying her son. "Regardless, they show some promise. Neither backed down once, which is possibly the most important thing—after the mechanical skill to land your strikes."

"*Mechanical skill* seems pretty important," Anna said, pouting slightly.

"Absolutely," Ešlija agreed. "But those who give up will never learn to improve. And underestimating an opponent is a sure way to lose. You must always be working, like how your Dādi is always working to solve a problem."

Anna looked up at Dādi. "Like when your hypo-these doesn't work—"

"*Hypothesis*," Dādi corrected her.

"When it doesn't work, approach the problem in a new way," Anna finished. "That's what you said about the thing you were trying to fix earlier."

"That's right. Sword fighting and engineering are very different, but both require a great deal of skill and the patience to learn it."

"I've got patience."

"You both do." Ešlija chuckled.

"And any time you want to test your patience"—Gustavs smiled at Justīne—"I'll be more than happy to beat you up and down the ring."

Justīne tore a piece of her rye bread off and threw it at his stupid face. Anna's laughter carried over Dādi's rebukes, and Ešlija stopped her son before he could retaliate in kind.

When Justīne woke the next day, she discovered no less than three purple bruises across her arms, legs, and chest. They were easily hidden beneath her clothes, but getting dressed elicited aches throughout her entire body. She grit her teeth, trying to stay quiet so as not to wake Anna, who still slept beside her.

Graudiņš asked her to help him in the greenhouse when she arrived. As the day progressed, light streamed in from the rooftop windows. The air smelled of rancid wet soil as they worked fertilizer into the pots and little gardens inside. It was a bit late in the season to be getting them prepared and planted, but it had taken a while to collect the barrels of dung, decaying leaves, and rotten food—which made up the fertilizer. Last year, they'd had help from Dzevrs and Zigmārs, the Lord Mayor and Beatrice's sons, but the elder boy fell ill over the winter. Dzevrs had only been nineteen. Just four years older than she was. His loss and the funeral pyre they'd made for him weighed on Justīne's mind as she and Graudiņš worked. She could almost hear the funeral song that Sofija had sung for him, a haunting tune about passing into the next life; ironically, it was one that doubled as a celebration of marriage.

Justīne noticed Ešlija walking along the wall's walkway, her sword at her hip and arquebus over her back. She crossed paths with Ievan, who was patrolling the walkway as well and walking in the opposite direction as her. Seeing him outside of his forge was a surprise, but perhaps the other guards were all busy, or he didn't have anything to work on today.

A part of Justīne was glad to see that Ešlija had taken her points about the gaps in their defense seriously. She was also disappointed that Ešlija was putting her and Anna under such close guard. It was important to always have at least one guard on duty, in case an atstrumeter failed or the maalkonis surged forth, but they only needed one person to do that. Nothing had ever come out of the maalkonis. No, she was just keeping her and Anna off the wall, which was ridiculous as far as Justīne was concerned. They would keep their word. It happened that nobody *hadn't* told them not to climb over the wall before. At least, not that she could remember.

At midday, Graudiņš announced that he was off for his repukdau prayer and meal, a process which often lasted several hours. The old man took his time most days and often had a nap afterwards. Lately, Justīne had been using the time to sneak off with Anna to check on the robin's nest, but that was no longer an option. Even so, her sister came to visit shortly after the old man went into the farmhouse.

"It stinks in here," Anna said, stopping to pet Pūka. The cat arched her back, nuzzled Anna's fingers, and then ran off.

"It stinks, but it's good for the plants. I'm almost finished. Besides, I think the old man wants me to start planting soon. So, I'm almost done here, thank the Gods. You can wait outside if you want to stay away from—"

"Guess what?" Anna interrupted her, grinning. Justīne noticed that she was holding something in her jacket.

"Did Dādi have you bring me something to eat for repukdau?"

"No." She giggled. "Dādi doesn't know about this."

Justīne glanced up from the soil she was kneading. "What have you done?"

She presented the copper device that Dādi had been working on the day before. The unfinished one with a trigger and no casing.

"You stole that?"

"I *borrowed* it," Anna whispered.

"What even is it?"

"I call it an atstru-torch. It's like an atstrumeter, but it has a trigger and handle like the guards' arquebuses. Rather than repel the darkness like a wall, it lets you see through it. Like a torch!"

"Why… What is happening, and how do you know all this?"

"Dādi told me about it yesterday. Well, he told me what he hoped it would do. I told you I was going to ask him to teach me engineering things. He worked on this all day yesterday, and he described how all the parts worked while he did. It's a good thing engineering is fun, because *he* sure isn't."

"Anna." Justīne sighed. "You should bring it back before he notices it's missing."

"Dādi left for repukdau with Ešlija. Then he said he was going to try and repair a squeaky gear on one of the atstrumeters on the south wall. He'll be gone until last dim." She pouted, her arms going slack. The atstru-torch struck against her lap. "I like Ešlija, but you don't think Dādi's going to marry her, do you?"

Justīne shrugged. "I don't know. Seems like *she* probably wants to. I doubt she's trying to help train us purely out of the goodness of her heart, and she keeps showing up like moths on rotting fruit. But ultimately it's his choice. Not ours."

Anna crossed her arms.

"Just be glad that it's not Lilija," Justīne said.

"I like Lilija's chickens. And the cows."

"Yeah, but how do you feel about *Lilija?*"

Anna made an ugly face, scrunching her nose and pursing her lips. "The chickens are nicer than her."

Justīne laughed. She finished working the fertilizer into a large pot. When that was finished, she took off her gloves and set them on the rim of the pot. Justīne walked out of the greenhouse and found a small pool of water in the ground outside where she rinsed her hands and washed her face.

"I don't know how you stand it in there all day," Anna said, wrinkling her nose at the greenhouse.

"Graudiņš does most of the work in there. I just help when he needs it. And the smell fades quickly enough, though I'll admit that my first year with him was challenging." She nodded at the copper device her sister still held. "You're not bringing that thing back to Dādi, are you?"

"Nope." She smiled. "He said he still needed to test it, so I thought I'd do that for him. And it *works*. Better than I think even he expects. You want to see how it works, too? You'll never believe what I just hypothesized."

"I don't think that's…" Justīne sighed. "Sure, Anna. Show me what it does. Then repukdau right after. I'm starving."

"Follow me," Anna said excitedly.

Before Justīne could ask what for, she ran off. Justīne jogged after Anna, following her away from the greenhouse and the rest of the town. She leapt to the side to avoid ramming into Bruno's cart full of barley as he came around the corner. The man shouted something at her at the same time Justīne yelled an apology, not daring to break her stride.

Anna led Justīne into the hills. The forest that clung to the northern part of The Old Town had once been thick. She could almost remember the dense pines and oaks, many of which had been reduced to stumps—an unfortunate necessity of several especially cold winters as of late. Around their remains sprouted several saplings, some taller than Justīne, a blend of natural growth and Ievan's work.

Before the old blacksmith died, his apprentice had been adamant about making sure they planted trees to replace the ones they cut. Ievan didn't have much time for that anymore now that he was in charge of the forge, and apparently helping Ešlija with the midday patrol. Lately, she'd noticed Staņislavs taking up the effort in the smith's stead, gathering acorns and pinecones and other seeds from the forest floor and planting them. She looked around for him, but he must have been busy elsewhere.

Justīne hurried to catch up to her little sister. The ground became muddy, and her boots slipped over half-rotten leaves and twigs. Anna ran ahead, her dress skating between the trees as she used the stumps to leap over particularly wet stretches of ground.

"Where the hells are we going?" she called after Anna, hoping that she was out of earshot from anyone in town. If they were caught with a stolen atstrumeter—or whatever it was Anna had taken—that would be even *worse* than getting caught outside of the wall.

"Hurry up," was all that she shouted back.

The northern stretch of the wall loomed close by, its bricks falling into even more disrepair than those on the south end. The atstrumeters which lined it whirred all the same, holding back the maalkonis as their droning song filled the air. The wall's shape was jagged, following the odd forms of the hills which ebbed and flowed without rhythm. Some parts appeared to have risen or sunken over the years as well, causing parts of the structure to arch or collapse. Justīne was surprised that it hadn't broken apart yet.

Anna finally stopped near a portion of wall which had been built on a hill taller than most. Its base had crumbled, creating a gap in which cobwebs caught dust in the air. It was pitch-black inside, without even a hint of the midday sun touching anything beyond the aperture.

"What's this?" Justīne asked as both she and Anna caught their breath. "I've never noticed it before."

"It's the *tunnel*," she said, as if that was supposed to mean something to Justīne.

"What kind of tunnel?"

Anna shrugged. "I don't know. But do you see the leak in the surface there?"

Justīne peered into the dark. As her eyes adjusted, she began to see faint wispy shapes in the tunnel, like ink in water. She caught it glimmering specks of violet. "That's the maalkonis." She took a step back. "Gods. It breached the wall."

Justīne stared into the inky darkness, unable to catch her breath any longer, feeling as if somebody had driven their boot into her gut. This was the kind of thing everyone worried about. Every nightmare she'd had was about the maalkonis getting past the walls one way or another. And here it was, happening right before her eyes.

"Get away from there," Justīne told Anna, her voice quivering. She wanted to rush forward and pull her little sister back from it, but her feet were frozen. She couldn't move.

"It's not moving at all," Anna said. "It stays in the tunnel. The atstrumeters must work against it even when it's underground. I already hypothesized that."

"That's not how you use that word, Anna! Godsdamn. And how are you so relaxed about this? This isn't good. We need to tell Dādi."

Anna frowned. "It's okay. It's safe. Well, as safe as death mists can be. I found it at first dim and watched it while you were on the farm. I threw rocks and grass inside, tried—"

"You were *playing* with it?"

"I was testing my theory. And it never changed once. It's stuck there. The atstrumeters are still affecting it even below ground."

Justīne shook her head. "We have to tell Dādi."

"He'll just wall it off."

"*Exactly*. That's the damned point."

Anna frowned. "But aren't you curious to see what's inside, June?"

"We are *not* going inside there. The maalkonis will take us. We'll get lost at best, and at worst… Do you remember what happened to Monika? You were so young then, but I remember you were there too."

"I remember. Parts of it, anyway. That's why I brought this." Anna lifted the copper device she'd been carrying, the thing she'd called an atstru-torch, her finger wrapped around the trigger. Before Justīne could stop her, she raised it toward the tunnel and squeezed.

Two things happened at once. First, the gears inside spun, and Justīne heard a shrill sound emit from the device, not too different from the atstrumeters along the wall. She saw the inky blackness shudder at it, even in the darkness. Second, a copper wire at the end of the device began to burn a dim orange-gold. In the darkness of the patchwork forest, it was enough to illuminate the maw of the tunnel. Justīne saw how the maalkonis receded away from them, recoiling at the light like it hurt to the touch. The darkness still lingered, but when Anna took a step forward, it receded by equal measure. When she stepped backward, the maalkonis also came closer, filling in some of the space.

"Gods," Justīne whispered.

"So, can we have a look around?" Anna asked. "I—I don't want to go in alone."

Justīne knew that they should turn back, but watching the maalkonis recede so quickly stirred something in her. She'd never seen it react to anything like this. And she did wonder what lay beyond the walls; she couldn't even imagine what some of the adults talked about when they recited their great-grandparents' stories of not only the surrounding area but of other towns and *kingdoms*. Whatever that meant. They spoke of mountains and ox and all kinds of strange things that seemed impossible to Justīne. But if Anna could keep the darkness away with that device…

Justīne took a step forward. "Hold on to that torch, and stay close," she told Anna and put a nervous hand on her back. "I mean it. If anything happens in there, I can't protect you. You and I are just *gone*."

"I know," Anna said and stepped in beside her.

Justīne took a deep breath. Together, they delved into the tunnel. *Into* the maalkonis. It receded away from them with every step they took. The light Anna's torch gave off illuminated the tunnel's hollowed ground—though there was not much to see other than mud and stone. After a few paces, Justīne glanced back the way they'd come. The aperture was a bright circle against the dimly lit tunnel. As they continued into its depths, the maalkonis bent and reformed behind them until the way forward was just as dark as the way back.

"Glad there's only two directions," Justīne whispered, in case speaking too loudly might disturb the dead—or anything else that might live in the maalkonis. She'd long wondered if anything could survive beyond the town. It always seemed a fantasy, but Dādi had clearly created a device that could protect them from it, and Anna had learned to use it without issue. Had anyone else come up with a similar tool? Perhaps there were other towns out there, people like them who repelled the maalkonis, and all they had to do was find each other.

The torch allowed for a sanctuary of about two meters around them. Enough for them both to walk somewhat comfortably, but little else. The maalkonis formed and shifted around them, parting to allow their entry deeper into the tunnel and folding over the path behind. The device's clattering song sounded strange inside of the tunnel, where it echoed off the walls. Justīne tried to ignore it and be alert for any other sounds, should they come.

The tunnel ended in a wall of old brick, too far to be a part of the wall above ground. This was… Something else. Along the wall, the path split in two directions.

"Let's go left," Justīne said. "Just help me to remember that we turn right here to leave."

Anna nodded and continued deeper into the tunnel. She could feel her heart beating, pounding against her chest, but she kept moving. With the torch to protect them, this place seemed to be nothing more than dirt, stones, and bricks. Hardly the stuff of nightmares. Still, she clutched Anna close to her side, terrified of what they might reveal with each step.

They hit another fork in the path. This time, Justīne found a stone and slammed it into the bricks, marking it with a grey line where she'd struck them. When she was finished, they turned right. Justīne kept the stone in her hands, feeling a little safer just by holding the heavy thing.

They approached a third fork in the tunnel, where a wooden door stood between the paths. It seemed old and had been burnt along the edges, affixed on large rusty hinges. Justīne was beginning to worry that they'd stepped into a maze. If they took too many more turns, they'd risk getting lost. Besides that, the air in the tunnel was beginning to get to her. The pungent, earthy odor was almost comforting, but the way the brick and stone pressed in toward them from all sides made her nervous, and the maalkonis seemed like it was inching closer.

Anna tugged on the door's handle, but it only rattled in place. "It's locked."

Justīne wondered if somebody had locked it before the maalkonis took these tunnels. Or had *something* locked it afterward? Justīne was about to suggest they turn back when two violet lights appeared down one of the paths, a dim light in the dark.

"What's that?" Anna whispered.

"I don't know."

Anna took a step forward, and a shape around the lights came into view. It was blurry and dark in the maalkonis, but it was definitely human. Or, rather, human-like. The arms were too wide, and the body oddly slender. Everything about it seemed both familiar and *wrong*.

Justīne inched forward, her hand held tightly onto Anna's. The shape receded, and they advanced toward it slowly. Justīne thought about turning back, but her curiosity got the better of her. She tossed her stone near the lights. It clattered against the brick and dirt loudly, echoing, and a person lunged at them.

The lights, two violet eyes, burned through the maalkonis. Arms, longer than what seemed natural, clawed toward them, their shape obscured by long black feathers and bones that sprouted from the creature's forearms. Its screech was even more shrill than the whirring gears of the device that Anna held.

Anna screamed.

"Run!" Justīne shouted. She spun on a heel and sprinted, dragging Anna along. "Hold on tight!" she said, clutching Anna's hand.

The maalkonis was mere inches from Justīne's face. Her footsteps echoed in the tunnel, her heavy boots slamming into the mud and sliding over the stones. When they reached the dashed wall, Justīne turned left, charging down the black tunnel. The creature screamed at them, and she chanced a glance back at it.

The feathered creature thrust an arm into their bubble of light and pulled at it like the light itself was some kind of fence that could be ripped apart, a sheet that could be torn to ribbons. Its claws flailed and tore through it, every step and swipe coming closer to them. It stared back at her, its teeth bared in a fanged snarl, its eyes devoid of any emotion whatsoever. It made her heart rattle against her ribs, and she ran so hard that her lungs burned. Still, she refused to stop.

"Right!" Anna shouted.

Justīne noticed the first fork in the tunnel they'd come to and turned right there. They couldn't see the exit, but if they retraced their steps right, the maalkonis should part just up ahead. Justīne pulled Anna along faster. She heard her sister—and the creature—sprinting behind her. Breathing. She felt something hot on her neck as the creature exhaled, snarled. Then a sharp pain in her back.

They spilled out into the midday light, collapsing beyond the tunnel's entrance. Justīne took the copper device from Anna and thrust it back toward the tunnel where they'd been. Somewhere in it, the shape of a person glared back at them, just beyond the light's edge. Their violet eyes blinked slowly and then disappeared into the dark.

Anna began to cry.

Justīne turned the torch off and cradled her sister in her arms. She shook, her breathing too haggard to form words. They had made it. There were creatures on the other side of the maalkonis. One had found them, but they'd outrun it. All of her nightmares were real, and they'd still escaped. She collapsed over her little sister, sobbing, and tried to thank the Gods, but the words came out in an incomprehensible mutter. She stuttered over them and gasped for air, her lungs on fire and her muscles aching. Her back stung and was drenched in sweat.

Despite all that, she felt the sun on her skin and could hear birds chirping in the trees. It seemed so bright and warm compared to the complete darkness inside of those tunnels. The creature, whatever it was, hadn't pursued them here. Just as they were tied to the light, it was locked into the dark. She didn't understand why, but she knew it instinctively—or perhaps the alternative was simply too frightening to consider.

"You're hurt," Anna said through her tears.

"What?"

"Your back."

Anna touched her back and pain stung down her spine. Justīne cried out. When she looked at her fingers, they were red with blood.

"I'm sorry," Anna said. "This is all my fault."

"It's okay," Justīne lied. It was damned *not* okay, but now wasn't the time for that. She touched her back and felt for the wound. It was high, just below her neck, and trailed as far as to her right shoulder. "How bad does it look?"

Anna thought for a moment, finally getting her breathing under control. "It doesn't look very deep. It's bleeding, but… But I don't think it's too bad."

"A shallow cut, then?"

"Yeah."

"That's good, at least. Damn. My tunic?"

"It'll need mending, but I think you and I can fix it. It'll be stained from the blood, though."

"Okay. I'll get a change for now. And I'll go see Sofija later to make sure it's not infected. She probably has a poultice or something I can put on it."

"Does it hurt?"

"Like a bee sting," she lied. It wasn't that bad, but it was definitely worse than a bee sting.

Anna winced.

"We have to tell Dādi about this," Justīne said. "He will know what to do."

"But he'll know I stole his torch," Anna sniveled.

"He'll forgive you."

"You don't understand." Anna pushed against her. "I hate all of the little jobs everyone here has. I hate that you have to shovel dirt and poop for the farm. I don't want to cook or clean or be sweaty in the forge or walk around the wall for hours every day just waiting for the maalkonis to kill us all, and I *hate* Lilija's stupid face. I wanted to become a mage so that I could make the dark go away, but there's nobody to teach me anymore. Engineering is all that's left. And Dādi won't teach me if he doesn't trust me."

Tears formed in the corners of her eyes, but her glare was deadly serious.

"Please don't tell him," Anna pleaded. "We won't come back. We can even get some shovels from the farm and bury the tunnel if you want. The maalkonis isn't getting any closer and neither is that *thing* in it. It would have followed us out if it could have. Let's just put Dādi's tool back and get something to eat. Okay, June?"

Justīne sighed. At the mere mention of food, her stomach growled. She stood and helped Anna up as well. Dirt rubbed between their hands.

"I'll bury it as soon as I can sneak away with a shovel. Once that's done, we can never come back here," she told Anna. "And we can't tell anybody about what we did."

Anna nodded.

"Promise me."

"I promise."

"Good." She took a deep breath. "We always knew there might be things out there. I suppose now we know, and we know they can't get in."

"That's right," Anna said. After an uncomfortable silence, she added, "Maybe we should say an extra prayer at repukdau, though. Just in case."

"Yeah." Justīne took her hand. "It couldn't hurt."

II

Two years later...

Graudiņš' funeral pyre cast a long trail of smoke into the sky; macabre scents of burning wood, daisies, and flesh mingled in the air. Justīne watched the flowers curl between logs, wilt onto the stones below, and crumble to ash as the flames took them.

Beatrice led a prayer for the farmer. Everyone who was in attendance, nearly the entirety of The Old Town, responded in unison. They were just over one hundred, or thereabouts, gathered in the cold winter air. Snow crunched underfoot and dusted their cloaks. A passing was not rare in The Old Town, especially among the elderly. Even so, each was a great loss, and this winter had already been harsh. Graudiņš would be missed. As much as he could be a pain in the arse, he'd always been there, had always provided for the Ļaodil.

The old man's cat nuzzled Justīne's leg. She bent down to lift Pūka up, but the little beast hissed at her and ran off behind Ievan's forge. How that miserable thing had outlived its master, Justīne would never understand. Graudiņš used to say that Pūka could fight Death themself.

The final part of Beatrice's prayer was not for the old man but for Justīne. The baker prayed for the Gods—she mentioned Thirst by name—to support her and grant her a bountiful harvest this year. All eyes shifted toward Justīne, surely considering the same uncomfortable truth. From now on, until she took on an apprentice of her own, only she would work the fields. Though they had received help on occasion from different people, especially during spring and autumn, Graudiņš had not taken on any other apprentices. How could he after he grew so ill?

What was it that Graudiņš had told her once? Something about how the walls and atstrumeters meant nothing if they could not feed themselves. The old man never said it quite so eloquently as that, but in death he seemed a wise sage—and perhaps a bringer of dark omens.

Perhaps Pūka could help her fight those, too. Although, she was certain that the cat didn't like her. It was just as likely she'd lure dark omens to Justīne. The cat might not even ask for a treat afterward.

Despite herself, Justīne smiled, caught up in her little fiction. Her lips fell as Beatrice finished her prayer.

The pyre was still burning as Staṇislavs and Sofija stepped forward from the attending crowd. Staṇislavs was dressed handsomely in a white cloak with red trim, stained slightly by age and smoke. His sister, Sofija, was in a beautiful flowing dress and draped in a heavy wool cloak. Together they sang an old hymn, a tune that Justīne had heard at every wedding, funeral, and sometimes in passing as her neighbors worked. Others joined in, their voices mingling together in the winter air. She didn't know most of the words, but she hummed along with the verses and whispered the choruses. It seemed as though everyone in The Old Town was singing along, the song swelling with each chorus. Staṇislavs and Sofija could hardly be heard, their voices folding into the rest. It was said that singing—it didn't matter much what song it was—could help a soul reach the afterlife. If that were true, Graudiņš had certainly found the Bright Garden.

As the song ended, people began to return to their work or homes. Many of them stopped to pat Justīne on the shoulder or utter some well wishes to her. Ievan and Bruno offered their condolences. Beatrice told her to remember her prayers, and her husband the Lord Mayor reminded her that The Old Town was right behind her. Staṇislavs touched her arm and said a few kind words about Graudiņš then quickly retreated into the crowd. Lilija stopped long enough to tell her that she should go visit Uli the bull sometime, which was about as close to a kindness as the woman seemed able to muster.

Ešlija, who was Justīne and Anna's *Pamaman* now that she and Dādi were wed, told her to call upon them if she ever needed help. Gustavs, her new brother, gave a little nod. It wasn't much, but she'd come to know him well enough to understand he wanted to say more; he just didn't have the words. She nodded back at him.

As the crowd thinned, Dādi and Anna remained at her side. They simply hugged her. Their embrace was uncomfortably tight, but she didn't want them to let go. She held them close and was thankful that they couldn't see the tears in her eyes.

❧

"Dādi, how old were you when your master died?" Justīne asked.

"Not much older than you are now." Dādi paused then put down the atstrumeter he'd been repairing. He hesitated, weighing his words. Finally, he said, "It was a frightening winter. Many people lost their lives. You know, there used to be *thousands* of people in this town.

My grandfather once told me how there was barely enough room to fit everyone when he was a boy. Many families all slept in one room, sharing the building with five, ten other families. But this was many years ago, and the years have not been kind. One particular winter, when I was about seventeen or eighteen years, an illness spread through us. Resources became scarce."

"People turned on each other."

It wasn't a question. Dādi and Ešlija no longer softened their stories the way that they'd used to around her and Anna. The Old Town had a history of bloodshed long before the maalkonis arrived, and since then, it cycled between bouts of peace and division. It was stupid, and Justīne could hardly imagine such a thing, but Dādi and Pamaman assured her that at a certain point hunger and desperation could drive anyone to violence.

"They turned on each other," Dādi confirmed. He spoke quietly. "My master engineer, Timurs, was struck through with a spear. He'd tried to break up a fight over some bread, but the thief was angry, and the guard who caught him had been drinking. We couldn't stop the bleeding.

"The Lord Mayor held a vigil for three nocti. Back then, engineers were seen as a kind of mage—except *we* had actually found a way to halt the maalkonis. Not only was Timurs well-liked, but without him, there were only two of us left to protect the town from annihilation.

"Timurs' death hit everyone hard, but it had a kind of sobering effect. The fighting came to a stop for a while, and everyone agreed to cast his murderer into the maalkonis. Some nocti, I can still hear that guard's wailing, his pleading for mercy. The silence that followed."

Justīne heard her sister snoring in the other room, resting peacefully. She wanted to go in with her and share the old bed as they used to, but she didn't want to wake Anna. Besides, it wasn't her bed anymore. It hadn't been for some time.

"What happened next?" Justīne asked.

Dādi shrugged. "What could I do but continue my master's work? People looked to me and Karīna, his other apprentice, to make sure the atstrumeters ran smoothly."

The name sounded familiar, but Justīne couldn't remember the other engineer's face. "Did I ever meet Karīna?"

"Yes." He smiled. "I'm not surprised you don't remember her, you were both so young, but Karīna helped me raise you and Anna. After your mother passed... I couldn't have managed without her.

"Karīna's mother was a mage. She used to work with Monika and imparted some of that to her daughter. Karīna knew all these tricks that you kids loved. She could create a glimmer—a kind of illusion spell—which you were just entranced by. Sometimes, she made them in the shapes of animals, sometimes stars or trees… And Anna, no matter how foul a mood she was in, would always giggle and laugh at them."

"And she…" Justīne said.

"A terrible accident, I fear. Nobody ever found her body, but she went missing when you were young. We sent out search parties, but as you can imagine, nobody could venture very far."

"You think she left the walls?"

"I think so. Dimitraj found her scarf in the hills, but we never found out what happened to her. Where or why she gave herself to the maalkonis. If that was what happened at all."

The hills. Justīne eyed the box by Dādi's feet. In it were a collection of trinkets he'd been experimenting with over the years. Some had limited success; others were yet to work at all. Near the bottom was a pet project of Dādi's that he hadn't touched in at least a year, a tool that Anna once described as an *atstru-torch*.

Justīne still didn't understand what they'd seen in those tunnels by the hills, under and outside of the wall. That evening, she had snuck back with one of Graudiņš' shovels and threw dirt over the tunnel until it was blocked off. They hadn't spoken about it since they fled the place, except when Justīne told her sister that she'd buried the place.

Dādi was convinced the device he'd built was broken, and it was, though it was Anna who did it. She'd become his apprentice and learned enough about engineering to sabotage the project. It was for the best. Whatever was out there… Nobody needed to prod it. Justine still had a scar along her back, a reminder of that day. Ešlija had seen it one hot summer day and asked what had happened.

Cut myself on a nail at the farmhouse, she'd lied to her Pamaman. *Don't worry. It happened a while ago. It doesn't hurt anymore.*

"Graudiņš is irreplaceable," Dādi interrupted her thoughts. "But you do not need to replace him, June. You will handle the farms in your way with the knowledge that he gifted you, and one day soon, you will have your own apprentice to help out. After all, there must be two to any job of import in this Old Town. Somebody will step up."

"What if nobody does?" she asked. Though, privately, she wondered if she was even up to the task of teaching somebody about providing food for the whole town. She wasn't even sure if she could remember everything the old man had taught her.

"Somebody will," Dādi said again, more sternly. "The Lord Mayor will get anxious if you go on alone for too long. In the meantime, you can always call upon us. Your Pamaman and I, as well as your siblings, will not let you struggle. Not too much, anyway."

"Thanks. I should get some rest."

"Of course. *Lavekzīme*. Luck be with you."

"*Lavekzīme*," Justīne echoed back.

During the last few months of Graudiņš' life, Justīne had moved into the farmhouse so that she could help care for the old man and be closer to the farm. Not that it was a long walk from Dādi's home.

Returning there at last dim, it struck her that the old place was *hers* now.

Justīne stood in the darkness of the old house. Everything was quiet, save for a distant patter of Pūka's paws as the cat ran from one room to the next. A gentle breeze that leaked in through the windows, chilling Justīne's arms.

When nothing woke her up from this nightmare, when she felt dizzy from the duties she'd stumbled into, she went to the spare room and collapsed onto the bed.

❧

Most of the work that she and Graudiņš had done during winter had involved maintenance of the farm and their equipment, preparing for spring. However, they'd kept a few crops that could withstand the cold. The greenhouse was not much above freezing, but that was usually enough for the cauliflower, cabbage, and a few other crops. Some, such as the fava beans, could even survive out in the open if she suspended a covering over them to keep the snow and ice off. They didn't grow as large or as quickly as they did during warmer seasons, but they helped ease the pressure on the prior year's harvest and Lilija's livestock. And it was nice to have a little fresh food in winter.

Justīne watered the plants at first dim as the birds began to wake and sing. She spotted a few watching her from the tree beside the farmhouse, their feathers grey and eyes ringed in yellow. One of them cooed at her then flew off toward the old cathedral.

Her fingers were raw and red by the time she was done. Some of the water had splashed from the bucket and had soaked into her gloves. Between trips to the well, she exchanged them for a dry pair and watered the remaining crops more slowly. If she made that mistake again, she could switch to Graudiņš' old gloves, but she couldn't bear the thought.

By midday, Justīne began taking stock of what remained from last year's harvest, marking the quantity of each fruit and vegetable in the farmhouse's cold cellar—something that neither she nor Graudiņš had gotten the time for this year. Justīne had spent every moment tending the crops, transporting them into town, or caring for Graudiņš.

The underground storage was larger than the farmhouse above it, filled with shelves and racks and barrels of food. Some of it was recently renovated, modified with additional places to store tools during harvest season when space was limited. As it was, in the heart of midwinter, there were pockets of empty shelves and hollow barrels. Nothing to be worried over, but Justīne was adamant about keeping good records. Her master had never been too interested in it but he had always seemed to appreciate her work. When they understood what they had in stock, they could make better decisions about how to divide up the food and what to use it for, what to dry and save for later.

She took a quill pen and made note of everything, methodically working her way from the back of the cellar to the front. As she did, Justīne found an apple on the verge of rot, its flesh soft to the touch, and bit in. Better a snack now than left to waste it later. The fruit's flesh was cold, mealy, and bitter, but she'd had worse.

Justīne was nearly a quarter of the way through their stores when she found a few mouse droppings in the corner of the cellar, near a barrel of beans. She dug through it and found nothing out of the ordinary. She checked another barrel nearby and, upon lifting the cover, found three small brown mice. They scurried away faster than she could react, slipping through a hole in the side of the barrel and then scattering. Justīne started after one, but the creature was already gone.

She investigated the hole in the barrel. It looked as though the mice had chewed through the wood, given the way it was carved into a perfectly-sized circle to fit their bodies. Many of the beans inside had been eaten, and more droppings were mixed in with them.

Justīne checked another barrel of dried apple slices, which Graudiņš had kept in storage for Aleks, The Old Town's grocer. He helped to distribute food to those who needed it, but he also liked to dry and preserve fruits, which was helpful for winters. Aleks' dried apple slices were a favorite of hers—and the mice had gotten into them as well. The barrel was half as full as it should have been, and tiny droppings littered the surface.

"Hells," Justīne hissed and shut the barrel. "Where's that Gods-forsakened cat?"

A knock came at the door. Gustavs stood there in a heavy brown coat, his breath a wispy white cloud. He carried a small pot, steam rising from around the lid.

"Mama made soup," he said.

Justīne stepped aside, and her brother came in. He set the pot on a table. It took only a moment for her to smell the seasoned vegetables inside, and her mouth watered—though she was still too furious about the mice to get excited about the gift.

"How are you doing?" Gustavs asked, lingering beside the table.

Justīne took a deep breath. "I'm managing so far. It's only been a day since… And Graudiņš wasn't doing much to help in those final weeks. He didn't have the energy. Not much has changed."

"It has, though, hasn't it? There was always a chance he'd get better before."

Justīne nodded. She put her hands in her pockets to hide the way they shook.

"Hey," Gustavs said. "I didn't mean to stress you out. I'm trying to say… I know the whole family has given you their word that they'll help you, but everyone's busy. Padādi and Anna are working on the atstrumeters, and Mama never leaves the wall. I don't know what her obsession is with it."

"She guards against the maalkonis and anything in it." Everyone knew that.

Gustavs scoffed. "If the maalkonis surged forth, she would be taken by it. You know that as well as I do. No matter how skilled of a fighter you are, it takes you. There's nothing to fight against. No monsters hiding in it."

Justīne nodded, her mind wandering to the thing that she and Anna had seen two years ago. She could still see its purple eyes in the darkness.

He continued, "All I mean to say is that I don't really have a lot going on, and I can help you out around here. I'd *like* to help you. I'm bored of walking the wall and training at the ring. It's like watching snow melt. In fact, some days that's exactly what it seems like my job here is."

"Are you asking to be my apprentice?"

"Gods, no. I couldn't suffer the embarrassment of that. I'm just bored. And I don't really feel like my work as a guard is really helping anyone. Not like what you or Anna do."

Justīne smiled. "I can't promise this will be all that exciting either. This first dim, I nearly gave myself frost-bite, and since midday, I've been counting our stores from last year's harvest."

"Better than taking up Ievan's offer."

"What did Ievan offer you?"

"The creep asked me to help him around the forge."

"That makes him creepy?"

"No, but a week ago he asked me to *wed* him."

"I didn't realize things were that serious," she teased.

"There are no *things* between us. He's having a hard time with that. When I declined his offer, Ievan went behind my back and asked Mama for my hand. She wasn't pleased. Refused to arrange it and said it was my decision, thank the Gods." Gustavs took a seat at the table. "I like Ievan, just not like *that*. We used to be friends. But then we both got caught up in our apprenticeships and kind of grew apart. He doesn't like being told 'no,' though. At this point, I wish he'd just leave me alone."

Justīne laughed. "Ievan's an idiot too, then."

Gustavs glared at her.

Justīne said, "He picked *you* to pursue like this, probably the best fighter in town. Seems like a risky bet to hound after you this much."

Gustavs smiled. "I don't know about that, but yes, I could beat him senseless. I wouldn't, though. But if he ever gives me reason to—"

"I've seen your work first-hand. Maybe pull your punches a bit. I know he's been showing Bruno's son around the forge, but that kid's far from ready to work as the principal smith."

"I promise, I wouldn't hurt a hair on his stupid little head," he said, raising his hands. "If he keeps coming after me, I may need to flash some iron, though." He patted the sword on his hip.

"Well, Ievan's a smith, so he might actually like that."

Gustavs groaned. "You're worse than your dādi."

A comfortable silence grew between them, and in it, Justīne's mind returned to the cellar, and her parchment that she'd left down there, scrawled with all of the contents she'd counted thus far. It was too soon to know for sure, but…

Justīne took a seat beside Gustavs. "I could use your help, actually."

"What's wrong?" he asked, sitting a little more upright.

"Could you count the inventory from the butcher and grocer? Whatever they still have in stock. Krišs and Aleks should be keeping track already, so you can probably just make a copy of whatever their most up to date list is. Tell them I sent you. If they ask why, I'm preparing their deliveries."

Gustavs frowned. "I don't recall Graudiņš ever doing that."

"He didn't."

"So, why am I collecting Krišs and Aleks' inventories?"

"Because I need you to."

He leaned forward, questioning.

Justīne swallowed. The words came in a whisper: "I don't know if there's enough food to last the winter."

"Stop."

"I'm serious. The last harvest was *fine*. Not great, but more than enough. But I just found that some mice got into a few things while I was busy taking care of the old man, and last I remember, Krišs and Aleks' orders weren't particularly conservative."

"When I offered to help, I thought you might have me water some plants or something," Gustavs said, dragging a hand down his face. "I'll see what I can find for you."

"Thank you. And don't tell them anything about this. I don't even know the extent of the damage yet, and I don't want to start a panic. At least, not until I know more."

"I understand."

"Perfect." Justīne ran a hand through her hair. "I also need to find that good-for-nothing cat."

Justīne never found Pūka. Instead, Pūka found her in the cellar sometime after she'd returned to taking inventory. The cat stopped beside the bundles of barley, blinked at her, and continued on its way.

"No vekrēla for you today," Justīne told her. "Get yourself a plump mouse or two, and we're even. Not a scrap until then."

Pūka swished her tail as she walked around a barrel of aged cheese. Thankfully, the mice somehow hadn't found it.

Gustavs returned before last dim. He let himself inside and found her in the cellar, two inventory lists in hand.

When he handed them over, Gustavs said, "Krišs seemed suspicious that you were asking for this. Aleks tried to request a delivery for more supplies, said something about wanting to bake cookies. Seemed like bad timing, so I told him I'd let you know and left it at that."

"Thank you, Gustavs."

"Yeah." He looked around the room. "Do you need help counting?"

"That would be amazing. Let me show you where you can get started."

It took a couple of days to go through her entire stock as well as the butcher's and grocer's inventories. The situation wasn't as bad as she feared, but they would need to ration some supplies in order to make them last throughout winter. Nobody would starve—but only if they were careful.

At midday, Justīne visited Lord Mayor Dmitraj. He was a large, broad-shouldered man with long grey hair and a braided beard. He greeted her warmly, his cheeks rosy from the hearth he sat beside. He offered her a drink, and when she refused, he tried to give her something that Beatrice had baked. Justīne declined that as well, though she desperately wished she hadn't.

She asked to speak at the next town meeting. He inquired what for. She hadn't expected the question, though she immediately knew that she should have. She didn't want anyone to worry, but if anyone ought to know it was surely their Lord Mayor.

He asked to see the damage for himself, as well as the inventories Justīne had collected. She had brought the latter, but to show him the damage, they had to visit the farmhouse. The Lord Mayor picked up his copper torch, and they left quietly, snow crunching underfoot. He turned away his personal guard when they began to follow him. They seemed confused about that but stayed behind as they were told.

Justīne showed him to the farmhouse cellar. The Lord listened intently, quietly, until Justīne had gone over everything: what they found, what they'd lost, and what she'd been able to salvage.

"This is not good," the old man said, stroking his braided beard, illuminated by the glow of his torch. His brow was creased, and his eyes were closed as he worked through the problem. "Our next meeting is in a week's time, but I fear that we need to begin rationing *now*. Otherwise, it will only be more difficult. I will call for a gathering to be held at last dim, after vekrēla. We'll let them enjoy one more meal before they are burdened with this.

"While we ration goods, I want to be kept informed of what supplies are going to which homes, to the butcher and grocer as well. It will be your responsibility to manage it all and to protect what's left from the vermin, but you can always count on me. If you run into trouble, come to see me, even if it is the dead of nocti. Do not let my guard stop you."

"Of course," Justīne said, suddenly anxious about facing her neighbors. It had only been a few days since Graudiņš' funeral, and things had already spiraled out of control.

"It may not feel like it right now, but you did well, Justīne," the Lord Mayor said, his glare stern but warm. "I cannot imagine the stress you are under, taking over for Graudiņš. His are big shoes to fill. But we can prepare better when we know that difficult times are ahead."

"When was the last time that *difficult times* weren't ahead of us, my Lord?"

The Lord Mayor cracked a smile. "What luck, then, that the Ļaodil are such a resilient people."

❧

Some sixty or seventy Ļaodil gathered in the old cathedral at last dim; Justīne thought that she counted at least one of each household. That seemed like a lot for a meeting held on such short notice. The cathedral was alight with the glow of a dozen copper torches, each mounted on the wall. A dozen pews faced the apse, a tall stained-glass window in the center. At midday, it would have glowed with the light of the sun, illuminating the image with reds, yellows, greens, and blues.

Just then, at the end of last dim, the image in the window was obscured by darkness and tinted by the color of the torch's orange light.

Beatrice and the Lord Mayor were near the front with their son, Zigmārs. They offered their guests drinks. Bruno was laughing with Ievan and a few others. Krišs and Lilija were seated near the front, discussing something in hushed tones. Justīne's family had come as well. She wondered if anyone would think that odd—she and Gustavs hadn't appeared at a meeting in months. Too often, they found these events slow and uneventful. Justīne hoped that would be the case today, though she expected the opposite. All together, their separate conversations echoed off the brick walls and resonated in the air around them.

After some time, the Lord Mayor stepped up to the apse. He took his place behind an oaken podium and called for silence. Justīne caught his wife putting a finger to her lips, miming silence to their son.

"Dmitraj," somebody called from the back of the hall, "isn't it past your bedtime, you old goat?"

Beatrice was quick to respond from her pew in the front. "I may have spiked his drinks with a bit of Bruno's ale." She laughed. "Somebody's got to keep him going."

Bruno shouted approval and stomped his feet from the pews in the back, and others in the crowd gave a hearty laugh. Justīne glanced over at the Lord Mayor, who seemed perfectly sober, though he didn't dispute his wife.

"When you elected me Lord Mayor all those years ago," he said to the crowd, "I hope you know that you were really electing my lady wife."

"Exactly," Sofija called out. "We elected *her*,"

Again, those gathered erupted into raucous laughter. Somebody followed up with a call for 'Lord Mayor Beatrice' to take the podium.

"Can we get on with this?" Lilija shouted from her seat. The cathedral fell into near-silence. "Tell us what have you called us here for, Lord Mayor, so that we may get on with our lives. Some of us have to wake before first dim."

The Lord Mayor nodded. "Indeed. I will be brief. Our neighbor Justīne has brought a concerning issue to my attention, and she asked for a moment of your time at our next meeting. I thought it prudent that we hear her *this* noctis instead. So, without further pageantry, I would like to invite her to speak to you all. Please refrain from interrupting her until she is finished, you unruly crows."

Another chuckle arose from those gathered in the pews. Somebody cawed like a crow, which elicited an even louder reaction. Justīne tried not to look at them as she walked from her seat to the apse.

"Don't let them get under your skin," the Lord Mayor whispered as they crossed paths. Then he took a seat in the pews beside his wife.

Justīne stood behind the podium. There was space on it for a book or some other parchment, though neither she or the Lord Mayor had brought any. Perhaps she should have. She stared into the wood grain then up at the pews. Some sixty or seventy people stared back at her in pregnant silence. Justīne had known that she might have to address them one day, but Graudiņš usually only did when he needed to recruit a few extra field hands during a busy season. She couldn't recall the old man having to do anything like this before. And so soon after she took over the farm…

She took a deep breath.

"Thank you, Lord Mayor," Justīne said, aware of how awkward her politeness was after the way they'd jeered at the man. She also knew that her words were too quiet. She cleared her throat and tried again.

"Thank you." This time Justīne heard her voice echo off the cathedral's brick walls. As the hall reverberated with her voice, one of the copper torches flickered. "I am sorry to take up a part of your noctis. Like the Lord Mayor, I will be brief."

She took a deep breath.

"Last harvest was not poor," she continued, "but neither was it a bounty. I was reviewing our inventory a few days ago when I discovered that some of the food in storage at Master Grau—at the farmhouse—was eaten and soiled by mice."

A collective murmur emanated from the crowd, and heads swiveled as people whispered to one another. Their words blended together into a quiet hissing, like a pit of snakes.

"I collected inventory lists from our butcher and grocer," she raised her voice to overcome the din of their whispers. "Assuming no deficiency in what we are provided from Lilija's livestock, and no issues with the winter crop, we will have enough to last the season. But only if we are careful and ration what is left."

"Rations?" Krišs called out, clearly appalled.

"How much was lost?" Aleks asked.

"How did mice infest your farmhouse in the first place, *girl*?" Lilija demanded.

Justīne carried on. "We will begin with a slight reduction to all produce deliveries, and the Lord Mayor has agreed a slight reduction to what each household may take for themselves. I will monitor our stores and adjust accordingly and work with Aleks and Krišs—as well as the miller—to make sure everyone still has plenty of food for each meal. We simply need to be more mindful about how we use our supplies.

"As for the mice, I don't know how they got in. I'm still looking into it, as is Graudiņš cat," Justīne added with a smile, but the crowd had no interest in hearing about Pūka. If anything, mentioning her seemed to make them even more angry.

"If we can't find out how they got in, they'll just keep eating," Lilija said.

"And they'll be a problem again next year, too," Ievan added.

"I agree," Justīne said. "I swear to you, I will find whatever hole they've chewed through and patch it with brick, copper, or iron if I have to. Once I find it, they won't get back inside."

Ievan rolled his eyes—even from so far away she could see it in the way he crossed his arms and tilted his head.

Justīne said, "All I ask is a bit of patience from you all, until the early harvest comes in. As soon as the weather warms, with Uli's help, we'll have the fields plowed and seeded as quickly as possible. Soon enough, this will all pass. I swear it."

After a moment of silence, the Lord Mayor stood up. "I think I speak for the whole town when I say that I appreciate your efforts, Justīne. I will lend you whatever aid I can, as will the rest of you." He spoke to the crowd. "While we cannot undo what has happened, we can help each other through the rest of this winter. The Old Town, and all of you, have endured worse. We will take care of one another, as we always do. As we *must* do."

Lilija was the first to stand. She gave Justīne and the Lord Mayor a long look then turned heel and stormed toward the doors. She shoved them apart, the doors creaking on their hinges, and stepped out into the noctis.

The town's mood soured over the following weeks. Justīne kept a detailed list of her stores and what she delivered to the butcher and grocer. She maintained close communication with Lilija about her livestock, despite the fact that the woman openly blamed her and the late Graudiņš for their predicament, calling them 'careless at best, saboteurs at worst.' Justīne tried not to take it personally.

Justīne caught Ievan sneaking around the farmhouse at last dim one day. The smith claimed that he'd come to see her brother, but something about the way he said it convinced her that the forge master wasn't telling the truth. Gustavs began to spend more time around the farmhouse, as did Ešlija, guarding it from anyone who thought it might be a good idea to rob the cellar. Dādi and Anna helped in their own way, crafting a lock for the farmhouse which they claimed was impossible to pick. Justīne carried the key on her person at all times and tucked it under her pillow while she slept.

The Lord Mayor checked in with Justīne often, inspecting the cellar and discussing ways to best ration supplies. He gave her a great deal of authority in the decisions they made, but the old man became a constant presence nonetheless: making slight adjustments to what deliveries would be made that week; urging Justīne to send slightly more or less to Krišs and Aleks; discussing how to best preserve and protect what was left and the necessity to keep morale high. Or rather, as high as they could manage.

He also kept Justīne informed on his conversations with their neighbors. Lilija had resisted the Lord Mayor's request to provide the butcher with more meat to make up some of the shortfall in other products. However, Bruno had agreed to brew less ale than usual, allowing more barley for the miller to make bread. He saved the ale that he did make for holidays, making sure there was plenty available for special occasions.

During one of their meetings, Justīne told the Lord Mayor about Ievan. She didn't know if he intended to steal from her, but she did worry he might be considering it. And if Ievan was considering going to such lengths, others may be as well. The next day, one of the Lord Mayor's personal guards began to keep watch over the farmhouse. Niklāvs stood watch for her regularly thereafter. Once when he, Gustavs, and Ešlija all stood guard around the farmhouse together, Justīne thought that the place looked like it was under lockdown. Her fingers brushed across the key Anna had made for her. Perhaps it *was* under lockdown.

Things had gotten so out of hand so quickly. Justīne's mind reeled at the events of the past few weeks, all of her time spent in the cellar in addition to her normal duties around the farm. At least the cauliflower was growing well. Their heads ballooned as if they were near to burst. She would harvest them the following day at first dim. She would set aside the majority of the crop for the town and save a head or two for herself to roast. She liked it with a bit of char.

It wouldn't do to just harvest them, though. She would have to make sure Aleks and the Lord Mayor knew so they could tell everyone. Under normal circumstances, she wouldn't bother, but Justīne needed something—anything—that might calm her neighbors. This wouldn't fix things, but hopefully it would help show them that she was trying.

At first dim, Justīne left the farmhouse, locking the door as she fumbled with a stack of baskets and crates. Niklāvs was walking up the hill to the farmhouse as she emerged from it, and she greeted the Lord Mayor's guard with a little wave.

"Lady Justīne," he said in response.

Justīne recoiled visibly at being called a *lady* but decided not to correct him. "*Gentlesir* Niklāvs," she said instead, overemphasizing the made-up title. "You've come to watch over my shrubberies again?"

He smiled. Niklāvs was about eight years older than her, about twenty-five if she remembered correctly. He was a tall, lanky man, but he walked with a sort of confidence that Justīne wished she had. He wore a sword and uniform similar to Ešlija's, though he wore more armor than she did. A steel gorget protected his neck, and he wore a padded shirt beneath his chainmail. A winter coat hung over his shoulders, dyed a rich brown, with a pelt lining the inside. It looked cozy and warm.

"Shrubberies," he repeated, tasting the word as though it were bitter in his mouth. "I think you have a knack for selling yourself short, Justīne. Humility is good, but in abundance it can be ruinous."

Justīne laughed. "*Ruinious*, you say. Careful, sir, you're on the verge of becoming like those melodramatic poets of old."

He arched a brow at her. "Aren't all poets melodramatic?"

"You don't deny it then." She laughed again. "As much as I appreciate the company, I cannot stand around all day. Either come with me to the greenhouse, or I will see you again when I am finished there."

He pursed his lips, his good humor fading away as he glanced past her at the building behind the farmhouse. "I am here to keep an eye on the farmhouse. So long as I can keep an eye on it, I don't see why not. Do you need help carrying those?" He gestured at the baskets in her hands.

"Yes, thank you," she said and handed him a few. "I'm going to be harvesting what I can of the cauliflower today. If you're still here when I'm finished, I'll have you help me carry them back to the cellar, if you don't mind."

He smiled. "It beats standing around in silence all day."

"My, you guards live such thrilling lives."

"Boring is good. If my job becomes anything else, it means something has gone terribly wrong."

Later that week, Justīne gathered a shipment for Aleks and Krišs. It all fit in just one wheelbarrow and a pack that she had already strapped over her shoulders, but it was exactly enough for another week. Perhaps a little more, if she could convince Aleks to dry some of the fava beans. It would only take him a little time to roast them by the fire, and then they could be used in any number of dishes as a filler, from pottages to breads. It shouldn't be too difficult to get Aleks' help; he enjoyed cooking. The only trick would be *how much* should be set aside for later? She guessed a few pounds, but their neighbors could get upset if they heard so much food was being withheld from their already-reduced rations.

With the wheelbarrow packed, she locked the cellar, and the key twisted in her hand.

"Hells," she swore.

The thin copper rod had been bent and looked near to breaking. She pocketed it and tested the door, making sure it had locked. It was, but she wasn't sure that she could open it again. Yet another thing to worry about—and to worry about who found out.

Justīne delivered the food to the butcher first, leaving him with a few of the vegetables people often gathered with their meat and a few dried spices that Krišs liked. Thankfully, there was no shortage of mustard or garlic. The mice hadn't taken to those as well as other things in the cellar. Krišs thanked her with a curt nod, eying her bags like a crow might ogle carrion.

Aleks was more welcoming. He helped her unpack everything, placing it in his storage room or on the shelves around the grocery floor. He came up with the idea to dry some of the fava beans without her asking, which was a relief. She didn't pry about how much to set aside for that. He had a better sense of how much food people were picking up than she did.

It was last dim by the time Justīne was finished. There was more to do, always more to do, but she stopped by Dādi's house on the way back. He and Ešlija asked how the farm was doing and offered to set an extra place at the table for vekrēla. Justīne was grateful but declined. She wasn't particularly hungry and had to get back to the farm.

"You can't starve yourself," Ešlija chided her.

Dādi said, "I know things are challenging right now, but if you keep working like this—"

"I'll be okay," Justīne interrupted her dādi. "How about I join you for dinner tomorrow?"

Justīne found Anna in her bedroom. It was hers alone, now that Justīne had moved to the farmhouse. She'd turned half of it into a studio. Her workbench was reminiscent of Dādi's, covered in copper and iron parts, black grease and oil stains embedded deep in the wood grain. She was tinkering with an atstrumeter when Justīne stepped in the doorway. The atstrumeter was torn apart, its innards splayed out around her: wires, cogs, coils, and pistons all inert. Anna looked as though she was furious with it, like she'd been sparring with the machine for hours.

Justīne asked her, "That a new one, or a repair job?"

"Repairs." Anna sighed. "Always repairs. I have some new atstrus in the works, but they're coming along slowly. Trying to build one that lasts longer, so I won't have to spend every other week untangling wires and replacing gears. Sorry, it's been a long day." The way she said that made Anna sound years older than she was.

"Mhm. I get that." She tried not to sound quite as haggard as she felt.

"I heard you turn down vekrēla."

"Yeah. I came because I twisted this." Justīne flashed the bent key at her. "I was hoping you could fix it, since you built the keys for that new lock. I'll need it by first dim, if that's possible."

"That's quick."

"It's the cellar key. If the Lord Mayor finds out I broke it, he might rethink all the trust he's put in me. If the others find out—Ievan and Lilija… I don't want to think about that."

Anna turned the key over in her hands. "I need to finish this repair first, but I can ask Dādi to get it back on the wall for me. I'll get this to you as soon as I can after that, but it won't be as soon as first dim."

"Sure," Justīne said. Repairing the machines that kept the maalkonis away *was* more important. But she hated being locked out of the farmhouse cellar. It just played into the narrative that she couldn't handle running the place. "Nothing you can do to fix it short term? I assume bending it back isn't good."

"There are some things I could try, but I can't guarantee things wouldn't get worse."

"Worse how?"

"Well, if all I do is bend this back, your key is probably going to snap off *in* the lock. Getting it out after could be tricky. The other option could cause a whole host of issues. You know"—she flicked her fingers at Justīne and whispered—"*boom.*"

Justīne furrowed her brow at Anna. Her little sister tapped something below the desk with her foot, and Justīne stepped back to get a better look. It was dark under there, but after a moment she recognized the familiar shape of Monika's books.

"Absolutely not," Justīne whispered. "I thought you got rid of those."

Anna grinned at her. "Dādi thinks so too."

"You're still reading them?"

She whispered back. "Of course I am. They're the only thing we have left of the mages. Even if I never figure out what to do with them, somebody else might need them one day. Monika was experimenting with something before she died. She had this amazing theory of something she called *rune pairs*, two similar runes that helped strengthen and stabilize one another. She had plenty of issues with them, wrote all about failed attempts, but in this one"—she kicked one of the books with her boot—"she had some better results with a different kind of ink. There's some relationship between the rune and the instruments used to write them. Monika was on the verge of *something* great, and Dādi threatened to *burn* her books if I kept reading them. Did you know that?"

"No, I didn't."

Anna rolled her eyes. "So, you can see why I kept reading them. He's always been so weird about magic, but it's a part of who we are. Just because Monika died doesn't mean we should throw away everything she'd worked on. For somebody who spends all day preserving this town for the future, fixing astronomers, he's so short-sighted."

Justīne nodded. "I suppose. But I don't think he's had a good experience with mages."

"What do you mean?"

"Well, Monika died drawing runes beside the maalkonis."

"And snow is cold. Yeah. Lots of people died because they lingered around the maalkonis too long." Anna shrugged.

"One of Dādi's friends was an engineer and a mage. He told me about her once, Karīna. Nobody knows what happened to her, but she disappeared one day. Maybe he thinks she drew a rune wrong or something. They never found her body."

Anna's eyes wandered. "I've never heard of an engineer-mage."

"I think she was mostly an engineer. But that doesn't change that all the mages he's known have had some kind of accident or something. At least, all the mages I know about. You can see why he'd be worried about you reading those."

"I suppose." Anna glanced back down at the key in her hands, feeling at the bend in the copper rod. "Okay, let me work on this atstrumeter, and I'll start on the key. I should be able to bring it back to you late tomorrow. Maybe the next day. That alright?"

"That would be amazing," Justīne said. "Just no runes."

"Don't tell Dādi I still have these books."

"I won't. Just… Don't hurt yourself. Dādi might be right to worry about it."

"Don't worry; I'm careful. Besides, I don't have much time to read them anymore." She held up the broken at-strumeter. "These ancient piles of scrap keep breaking."

Justīne frowned. "Should I be worried about the maalkonis?"

"No. We're keeping up with it. But that's why I want to build a better version. Eventually, something's going to break that neither Dādi or I can fix. Don't want to be caught off guard when that happens."

Each day seemed to get better, so long as Justīne stayed at the farmhouse. Her rotating guard of Niklāvs, Ešlija, and Gustavs helped keep her company while she worked. Anna fixed the cellar key and returned it without a word to anyone else.

The Lord Mayor called another town meeting, where he asked Justīne to report on how their food stores were holding up. She still hadn't found where the mice had snuck in from, but she also hadn't seen them get in again. Perhaps the cat had actually caught or scared them away.

Things were as good as they could be, but for many people at the cathedral that noctis, 'as good as they could be' wasn't enough. There was some squabbling. Teodor spoke above the others, a venomous frustration lacing his words. He complained of being hungry, and the Lord Mayor simply agreed.

"We're all hungry, Teodor," he said. "But I'd rather be hungry than starve. Wouldn't you?"

The next day, when Justīne delivered another shipment to the grocer and butcher, Kriŝs gave her the usual silent treatment. His son Teodor was there as well. When they locked eyes, he saw himself out of the room, still clinging onto the meat cleaver he'd been using before she'd arrived. When Justīne looked to Kriŝs for a little reassurance, he turned his back to her.

Aleks was, as usual, more pleasant. He was eager to help in what small ways that he could and showed Justīne the fava beans that he'd dried since her last visit. It was hard to express how thankful she was for his help.

As she left his place, she passed Ievan's forge. She kept her head down and maintained a quick pace on the road back to the farmhouse. She noticed Ievan watching her anyway, and how the smith whispered with Teodor. The butcher's son looked nervous. She hurried her pace.

Gustavs was keeping watch of the farmhouse when she returned. He was dressed in his town guard uniform, an old coat over his shoulders. She took a breath as she crested the hill, relieved to put some space between the heart of The Old Town and herself—and to have her brother keeping watch. She would never tell him that though. It would go right to his head.

As Justīne put the wheelbarrow away and stashed her pack, Gustavs stepped closer. "You have a minute?" he asked.

Justīne adjusted her cloak. "Depends."

"Everything's locked up?"

She nodded.

"Good. Come with me." He began walking back toward town.

"Why?" Justīne asked.

He stopped and spoke over his shoulder. "Humor me."

"I have things to do here."

"You always have things to do. Give me an hour. We'll come right back."

Justīne crossed her arms. After a moment, she followed him down the hill. One hour, she decided, was acceptable. As much as she felt a need to keep busy, there was really only so much she could do at the moment. Half of the winter crop had already been harvested, and it would be some time before the rest could be. She'd already watered them at first dim and midday, and she'd taken stock of the cellar's inventory before she'd delivered supplies.

Gustavs led her toward Dādi's home but walked past it, headed toward the eastern wall. Smoke from the charcoal hut nearby made the air smell sweet and acrid. They passed it, travelling further along the wall, until Gustavs brought her to the guardhouse and the training ring.

"I haven't been here since, what, last summer?" she mused.

The guardhouse looked empty. Gustavs produced a key from his pocket and unlocked the door. He returned with two blunted training swords.

"Don't tell me you dragged me here just to get your ass kicked," Justīne joked.

He handed her one of the swords. She hesitated.

"Take it," Gustavs insisted.

Justīne reached out and took the blade. It fit comfortably into her gloved hand.

"This winter's been shit," he continued. "I think it's been pretty difficult for everyone, but... Between Graudiņš' and the way people are blaming you for all this, I can't imagine the weight on your shoulders right now." Gustavs frowned and removed his sword belt, tossing aside his sharpened sword. "I can't fix any of that. But I remember how much you used to love coming here."

Justīne tested the weight of the sword, moving it slowly through the air. "I can't remember if I loved it here or if things were just simpler then."

Gustavs shrugged and took up a fighting stance. "Probably a bit of both."

"Probably." She matched his stance. "Ready?"

"Always."

Their swords met, and steel clattered. Justīne noticed his blade shift and his body lunge forward. Her arms were tired and sluggish, though, and he tapped her on the shoulder with ease.

"Still warming up," she said, stretching her arms as they reset.

"Warming up," Gustavs repeated.

They swing at each other again. Gustavs made the same move. This time, Justīne was ready for it and parried his blade out of the way. She swung back, and he twisted his body to the side, catching her sword with his. The blades slid across one another for a moment. Justīne angled hers and thrust, jabbing Gustavs in the hip.

"Ow," he complained.

Justīne smiled at him. "Looks like I still got it."

"We'll see," he said and readied up again.

They went on like that for over an hour, trading points in their duel. Neither of them was keeping close count, though Justīne was sure that Gustavs had twice the wins she did. He had been practicing for longer, and had all the finesse of a seasoned warrior, or so it seemed to her. But for all that fancy swordplay and footwork, she could still get a hit in. The longer they sparred, the more muscle memory kicked in, and she began to recall his tricks. After all, they'd fought like this off and on for two years. Anything he learned, she had to counter, and she had no difficulty parrying his sword so long as she could block it in time.

By the time they finally hung up the training blades, they'd long since discarded their coat and cloak. Swinging around blades, even in the dead of winter, was damned hard work. Sweat dripped down Justīne's hair and soaked her shirt. Gustavs looked the same, as though he'd gotten a bucket of water dumped on him.

As they walked back together, Justīne said, "Thank you. It was nice to forget about things for a moment, and just"—she chuckled breathlessly—"beat the shit out of my brother."

"I could tell." He chuckled. "You were less rusty than I expected."

"I know you're a better fighter than me, but I can't make it easy for you."

"Well, I pity anyone who thinks it's a good idea to cross you, June. Because I think a few of those hits are going to bruise."

"Hah. Perhaps one day, when I'm not chained to the farmhouse anymore, I'll join the guard."

"Gods, no," he half-grumbled, half-laughed. "Anything but that."

⁓

The next town meeting was attended by nearly everyone and ended in shouting. As did the one after that. By the following month, arguments became accusations. Lilija and a few others disagreed over how Justīne and the Lord Mayor were distributing supplies. Ievan, Teodor, and a few of the town guard wanted to place a guard of *their* choosing to supervise Justīne, as if Niklāvs, Gustavs, and Ešlija were conspiring against them somehow.

"Are you implying I'd steal from the cellar?" Justīne asked the smith, astounded at the suggestion.

He shrugged. "You're in the perfect position to do it."

"I'm trying to make sure nobody starves."

"It seems to me like you're just starving us."

"And pressuring me to slaughter my livestock," Lilija added. "Cows, chickens, and goats do not grow as quick as barley. I cannot simply slaughter them all, or we'll be in trouble for the years to come."

"Who is pressuring you to do any of that?" Justīne asked from her pew.

"The Lord Mayor," Lilija spat. "With your incessant *requests* to help supply people with eggs and meat that I cannot provide. And you with your *itineraries*. You all want me to help? Start by *not* handing over the whole farm to a *child*. This is her mess to clean up. I won't create a new one to help fix it."

"Lilija." Dādi stood up. "You're taking things a bit far, my daughter is doing—"

"If I hear once more about how that girl is doing her best…" Lilija interrupted, leaving the rest of her threat unsaid.

"How can any of us trust her?" Ievan shouted, his voice echoing in the cathedral. "How do we know that *she* didn't kill Graudiņš to get the farmhouse for her family? We all know she can wield a sword. You know, she's always talking about how *hard* she's working for us, but

I saw her and her brother sparring in the ring just the other day."

"Ievan," Gustavs warned him as the pews erupted into shouting.

"*You*," he turned on Gustavs. Justīne almost couldn't hear Ievan over the crowd's fervor. "I bet you helped her do it. I see now… It all makes sense. You found a nice cozy spot in the farmhouse and a whore all to your—"

Gustavs stepped forward and drew his sword, placing the tip on Ievan's chest.

The room went silent, and Ievan's face turned a ghostly white.

"Gav," Dādi said, his tone cautious.

"Put the sword away, Gustavs," the Lord Mayor said. "We can settle this peacefully."

"What happened, Ievan?" Gustavs growled at him. "You weren't always such a prick. Remember when we used to play at the training ring?"

Ievan swallowed hard, eyes locked on Gustav's sword. "You never let me win," he said, chuckling.

"Come on. We both know you wouldn't have liked it if I'd *let* you beat me." Gustavs frowned at him, all of the merriment drained from his face. The sight of it—how quickly his expression changed—sent a shiver down Justīne's spine. Gustavs continued, "We're not playing anymore. So, quit threatening my family. I won't ask again."

Beatrice stepped up to the boys and plucked the blade from Ievan's chest. Justīne caught sight of her son—eyes wide—watching from one of the pews.

Ievan was unharmed. All that the sword had left was a bloodless crease in his sweat-stained tunic. Still, he looked as though he'd seen a spirit. Good. A little fear in the smith's heart might help calm him down.

"I think we're done for today," Beatrice said. "Nothing productive can come when tempers flare like this. We should get some rest and return when we've all cooled off."

"I agree," the Lord Mayor said. "Return to your homes. We will have a special meeting next noctis—for the heads of each household only."

"So, we don't get a voice," Ievan breathed. He glanced back to the guards who'd been echoing him. "How many of you are the head of your household? One, two of you? The Lord Mayor means to silence us."

"That is not—"

"No," Ievan interrupted him. "I see where you stand now. These group meetings were a ruse from the very beginning, weren't they?"

"Quit it, Ievan," Justīne said. "He's only trying to help."

"Like your *brother* just helped, with a sword to my heart? Will you be next? Is that what you two were training for in the ring?"

"No," Justīne raised her voice. She did not want anyone to get hurt, but Ievan's incessant arguing was giving her a hell of a headache. The words spilled out faster than Justīne could think them through. "Although, Ievan, with every word you speak, the sword's sounding better and better."

"We're done here," Lilija said.

"We are," Ievan agreed.

They turned and left the cathedral. Others followed them until only half of the families remained, lingering in the hall. Among them were Justīne's family, Bruno, Sofija, Staņislavs, and a handful of other familiar faces. They looked at Justīne, then the Lord Mayor, fear in their eyes.

"I'm sorry," Justīne said, worried that she'd let her anger get the better of her.

"It's alright. We will sort this all out tomorrow," the Lord Mayor told her. Then to everyone remaining in the old cathedral he added, "We will make this right. I swear to you."

⁓

Justīne did not have a chance to speak with Gustavs before she left the cathedral. He'd left in silence before she had realized it. So, Justīne asked Niklāvs to walk her back to the farmhouse. He agreed without hesitation. He walked beside her, carrying a copper torch in one hand. The other rested on the pommel of his sword. She felt better with him around, though she still craved a sword of her own. She might have asked Ievan to forge her one, if she didn't think he'd stab her through the heart the moment he finished hammering it out.

Niklāvs seemed tenser than usual. His jaw was tight, and his eyes glared at the shadows around them as if they might lash out. Still, he walked with confidence, like always. She wondered what was going through his head but couldn't bring herself to ask him.

Justīne craved the light of first dim, a moment of normalcy in which she'd check on the plants and hunt down that damn mouse hole. She'd been so focused on calculating what rations to give out each week that she'd let the rodents slip by. Not anymore. Her top priority was finding and plugging whatever entrance they'd used to get inside the farmhouse. If she was lucky, she might kill a few and feed them to the cat. Or she'd find their bones. If she could manage any of that, perhaps things would go back to normal. They'd all still be hungry, but at least she could show everyone that it wouldn't happen again. Not under her watch.

"Try not to think too much about what happened back there," Niklāvs said, his breath forming white clouds that stood out against the dark sky of noctis. "Everyone's hungry and on edge. Ievan, Lilija, Gustavs… Everybody means well. They're just scared. It's easier to villainize somebody than acknowledge that things are simply out of their control."

"I know," Justīne said, though it was hard to sympathize with Ievan and Lilija. A part of her wished Gustavs had done a little more with his sword. She knew that it wouldn't have helped anything though.

She wanted things to go back to normal, but that wouldn't happen overnight. She needed to ease everyone's worries, but the fact was that they *had* to be careful. Justīne had only been in charge of the farm for a couple months, and it was all falling apart. She wasn't sure that she was cut out for it.

"I don't understand why they can't see that this is for everyone. Lilija should get it. Gods, she literally made the same argument about not providing more eggs and meat. I'm doing everything I can."

"I know you are," Niklāvs said, his voice steady. "I've seen you at work these past few weeks. You never stop."

She shrugged. "I'm just trying to live up to Graudiņš' legacy. His expectations. He would tell people the truth if he knew something was wrong."

"The old man refused to be subtle." The guard laughed.

"He didn't know how to be."

After a moment of silence, Niklāvs told her, "I will watch the farmhouse while you rest tonight. I think civility will return at first dim, but I worry that our neighbors may act out before then."

"Oh. Are you sure?"

He nodded. "There will be others keeping an eye on the Lord Mayor and his family. They won't miss me for one noctis. It is my duty to protect the Ļaodil, and tonight that means making sure you are safe too, Justīne."

Justīne nodded. "I'm sorry you got roped into this."

He smiled sadly. "When the Lord Mayor asked for one of us to help watch the farmhouse, I volunteered. I wasn't 'roped in.' I *chose* this. But I am sorry for you. This winter has not been easy."

"You volunteered?" Justīne asked. She glanced at him out of the corner of her eye, acutely aware of how her cheeks flushed with warmth. She didn't know if he would be able to tell in the torchlight, but she hoped not. "I thought the Lord Mayor told you to watch over the cellar."

"When the old man heard somebody was sniffing around the place, he and his lady wife were very anxious. It only takes one person to throw the whole town into chaos, you know. One hungry person acting selfishly can ruin everything we've built here. I think they were coming to the same conclusion as I did, but I said the words first: the farmhouse needed a guard detail. Nothing too oppressive. You don't want to make your neighbors anxious, and the Lord Mayor still needs his guard present. But we needed to dissuade anyone from making the mistake of stealing food. I offered to stand watch, and they agreed."

"I see."

"It's nothing, really," Niklāvs said, sounding a bit nervous. "We are in a tough winter. Whatever I can do to prevent it from becoming a *bad* winter, I'll gladly do. Just as I know you would."

They continued the rest of their walk to the farmhouse in relative silence, listening to the snow crunching between their boots and the road. Justīne's mind was a storm, struggling with what she could do to appease Ievan and Lilija, wondering if she should borrow and sharpen Dādi's old sword.

As they neared the farmhouse, Justīne fought the urge to invite Niklāvs inside.

When they finally reached the door, Niklāvs gestured toward it and said, "Get some rest. You have a meeting to attend next noctis."

That shook her out of her thoughts. "What do you mean? The Lord Mayor said that was for the heads of households only."

Niklāvs cocked an eyebrow at her. "Are you not the head of this house? Or is that the cat?"

Justīne looked at the old farmhouse. "I guess I'm still getting used to that."

"Change is a difficult thing, but it always comes. Whether we are ready for it or not."

She chuckled, fidgeting with her fingers. "I still sleep in the guest room. All of my stuff was already there from when I was taking care of Graudiņš', and…" She didn't know how to finish that thought.

Niklāvs was quiet for a while. He regarded the farmhouse, his lips drawn into a slight frown. "You will make it your own home in time. That won't diminish

Graudiņš' time here. He always knew that you would inherit everything. He had no children, and you were his only apprentice in the end."

"You're dangerously close to writing poetry again."

The guard smiled. "All I'm saying is that Graudiņš wanted you to have the place. The farm. He trusted you to have it. Wouldn't have apprenticed you otherwise."

Justīne took a deep breath to quell the tears that threatened to rise up. "Thank you, Niklāvs" was all she could muster.

"Good night, Lady Justīne."

As she went inside, Niklāvs put his back to the farmhouse and placed a gloved hand on the pommel of his sword.

Justīne shut the door behind herself and fell back against it. She leaned there for several seconds. She took a deep breath, and when her knees finally allowed it, she wandered toward her bed.

A crack of thunder woke Justīne from her dreams. It sounded close, which was odd for winter. She glanced out a window that looked out toward the hills in the north, and it didn't seem to be storming. Perhaps it had simply been part of her dreams?

Pūka leapt onto her chest, the cat's green eyes reflecting the light of first dim. Justīne raised a sleepy hand to pet the feline's head, and the beast swatted at her, baring long white fangs.

"Hells, Pūka." Justīne groaned and rolled her body enough that she forced Pūka to leap off of her. She heard the little beast sprint out of the room. For an old cat, she was quick.

Justīne dressed and threw on a warm cloak. She took a quick prausme of dry bread, muttering a sleepy prayer. She grabbed an extra piece to offer Niklāvs. Surely he'd be hungry, having stood outside all noctis. Then she filled her pocket with some of Aleks' dried apple slices to have later while she was in the field. After discovering the mice had gotten into them, she removed the top layer that they had eaten and tread all over. Justīne moved the rest to a more secure barrel, and she was craving something sweet.

Justīne made a small meal of the prior day's table scraps and set the bowl on the ground for Pūka. The cat ate a few bites, but then stopped and walked over to the door. When their eyes met, Pūka hissed at her.

"You're in a mood this morning, aren't you?"

Pūka blinked back at her.

Justīne slipped on her boots, and opened the door. As she did, Niklāvs collapsed at her feet. His eyes were glassy, and a bloody hole had bored through his chest. The damned cat leapt over him and dashed through the snow, her tail high and puffed up. Justīne lost sight of her as she looked out toward The Old Town, to where the cathedral was in flames. Its three towers burned like pyres against the dull grey sky. The sound of clashing swords and spears rang out as the sun rose. Just down the hill, a line of guards and townsfolk had formed, holding back a group who slowly advanced toward the farmhouse. They all carried swords, knives, or shovels. Two had arquebuses as well, but only one man seemed to be using it: Ievan. He was reloading it, shoving a ram rod down the barrel as fighting raged all around them.

Justīne pressed a hand to Niklāvs' wound, tears welling in her eyes. She muttered something incoherent, praying to the Gods for help. But his eyes stared back at her, unfocused and unblinking. His chest no longer rose or fell.

She shut the guard's eyes and made to speak a quick prayer to Death. She wanted to ask the God to make Niklāvs' journey to the Bright Garden an easy one, though the words failed to cross her lips. A confusing mix of heartbreak, shock, and fury raged inside her chest until finally Justīne took the guard's sword and scabbard off of him. It was heavy in her hands as she ran toward the fighting.

"There she is!" Ievan shouted from the opposite side of the line.

Justīne unsheathed Niklāvs' sword and walked toward the petty shrew of a man. She gripped it tightly, still holding the scabbard in her off-hand. She would finish what Gustavs hadn't.

People on both sides of the line shouted as Ievan leveled his arquebus at Justīne. A flurry of movement caught her eye—Ešlija. She charged forward, thrusting her blade into Krišs' side and slashing his son Teodor across the arm. Krišs collapsed there in the snow and mud, dropping his knife. His son dropped his sword and cradled his wounded arm, taking a step back and screaming. Ešlija stepped forward to strike at Ievan, but she was stopped by a pair of guards.

Ievan fired his arquebus. A puff of smoke erupted in front of his face, and a thunderous crack shook the air. Justīne kept walking. She didn't notice where the shot went. She didn't care to know.

Ešlija shouted a command. A moment later one of the guards beside her turned—Gustavs—and ran to her.

"Sheath the sword, Justīne," he said, his own blade in a tight grip. The steel was wet with blood and when he looked at her, his eyes drifted toward the corpse leaning against her front door. "You need to get out of here."

"I will stand and fight," she said, a furious tremble deep in her lungs.

She could hold her ground. Gustavs was the better fighter, but she'd been training with him and Pamaman since she was fifteen. If nobody else would run a sword through Ievan's guts, she would. And she'd make it hurt. Gods, she wanted to make it hurt.

"We can't find Anna," Gustavs said.

That stopped her in her tracks. "What?"

"Your Dādi went looking when the alarm bells rang, but I don't know if he found her."

Justīne hadn't even heard the blasted bells. She'd been sleeping while everything turned to shit.

"You need to leave, June," Gustavs repeated. "You're Graudiņš' only student. If we lose you, no matter who wins this day, we all end up starving. Besides, you know Anna best. We can't lose her either. The atstrus need to keep spinning."

Reluctantly, while Ievan reloaded his arquebus and the brawl continued around him, Justīne spoke to Gustavs, quietly. "To the hills."

"Good idea. We can use the height to our advantage."

"Yes, but if Anna is missing... Gods, I hope I'm wrong, but I know one place that she can go where nobody else would follow her."

"Lead the way," Gustavs said. "Mama and the others will hold them back."

Justīne heard another clashing of blades as she and Gustavs sprinted away. She dared not look at what she was leaving behind. She offered another silent prayer for Dādi and Ešlija and sheathed the sword as she led Gustavs past the fields, through the pockmarked forest, and into the hills. Once they reached a good vantage point, she stopped to catch her breath and looked back at The Old Town.

The fire at the cathedral had spread to the nearby buildings: people's homes and workplaces—even Ievan's forge. She was glad to see something of his burn, but she hoped nothing of import would be lost. They'd need it later, provided the Ļaodil survived this day.

She spotted other skirmishes in progress throughout the streets. A few people surrounded Lilija's house, where the woman was locking up the barn. A shout came from the town's gate, near the Lord Mayor's home. It was too far to see what was happening, but she spotted smoke rising that way as well.

"How did things get so bad so quickly?" she asked.

Gustavs put a hand on her shoulder. He said nothing, but Justīne could tell he felt the same pain as she did. It choked her, demanded to be felt, and beckoned some kind of reason for all this bloodshed.

She cut off the thought. It would overtake her if she let it. When she looked at Gustavs, she knew it would envelop him as well. Already, tears welled in his eyes, and his hands shook terribly.

"We need to keep moving," she said, leading the way further into the hills. "Otherwise, I'm going to march back down that hill and stab Ievan in his fucking throat."

The ground became mushy and wet as they neared the wall. Snow, and the dead leaves piled beneath it, crunched underfoot. Overhead, the maalkonis loomed, a dark and unsteady cloud. The sun cast hazy, uncertain shadows from the trees. She led Gustavs along the wall to where it ebbed and flowed with the jagged shape of the hills.

Anna stood beside the wall when they found her. She held a shovel, its blade damp with snow and mud. On Anna's hip, she'd strapped a copper device: the at-stru-torch she'd sabotaged. Beside her, the tunnel into the maalkonis, which Justīne had covered up two years ago, was freshly unearthed. Pūka was there as well. She sat on a rock beside the wall, tail curled over her paws.

When Anna saw them she ran to Justīne. She embraced Anna back, still holding Niklāvs' sword, as she hadn't had a moment to affix the belt around her waist. She wasn't sure yet that she wanted to. Anna still gripped her shovel, and Justīne felt a little soil fall on her back, but she didn't care.

"You found that Gods-forsakened cat," Justīne said. A laugh nearly rose out from her throat as they parted.

"What are you doing out here, Anna?" Gustavs asked her.

"If there's ever a time to leave The Old Town, I think this is it," she said, holding up the atstru-torch.

"I don't understand. I need to keep you two safe. We need shelter."

"Look," Anna told their brother and walked him to the black maw of the tunnel that led into the ground below the wall. "This tunnel leads outside of The Old Town. Something's down there. Evidence of people."

"People and monsters," Justīne said.

"What do you mean?" Gustavs asked.

"I mean, we need somewhere that those idiots won't follow us," Anna said.

"Hells," Justīne whispered. "Anna might be right. I don't like it either, but the maalkonis might be safer than anywhere inside the walls right now. Anywhere we hide in here, they'll find us eventually. And even if we can handle ourselves, Anna's no fighter."

"I'm not *that* bad," Anna argued. She glanced at the blade Justīne carried. "I seem to be the only one without a sword though."

Gustavs stared at them both. "Are you two mad? The maalkonis grinds you into ash. It has never done anything other than destroy things. You can't go into it."

"This will protect us," Anna said, indicating the copper device. "June and I have used it before. And I've been making improvements to it lately. It will last longer than it used to and project a wider area."

"I thought you'd made it stop working?" Justīne asked.

"I made *Dādi's* stop working. This one's mine. I made a new one based on his design, and it works even better."

"You didn't think to tell me about this?"

"You were always so scared of coming back here. I figured you wouldn't want to know."

"Of course I was scared of coming back. You remember last time?"

An arquebus fired in the distance, and a tree branch beside Gustavs erupted into splinters. It startled Pūka as well, who leapt off her perch and paced around their feet. Down the hill, Ievan and a few others—it was hard to tell how many through the gnarled trees—had followed them up the hill.

"Mama," Gustavs said, his voice cracking.

"We're out of time. We have to go," Anna told them.

"Hells." Justīne groaned. "Does it emit enough light to fit three of us?" She glanced down at the cat. "Four of us, I guess."

Pūka mewed at her.

"Plenty," Anna said proudly.

Gustavs ran a hand through his hair. "Gods, you two are actually insane."

"You don't have to come with us, Gustavs," Justīne told him. "But I think Anna's right. If we stay, there's a fifty-fifty chance we wind up dead. Ievan is coming this way *right now*. In there… I don't know exactly what's in there, but I do know that nobody would dare follow us in. Anna's got the only working atstru-torch. It will keep the dark away. In there we have a chance."

"They'll think we perished in the dark," Anna added. "They won't expect us to come back. Even if all we do is hide, we'll be able to surprise them when we return."

"Show me how that thing works," Gustavs said to Anna through gritted teeth.

"We don't have time for this," Anna grumbled, but she turned on the atstru-torch and held it toward the tunnel anyway. Just as it had two years prior, the maalkonis recoiled at it—though this time, its radius must have been at least twice as wide.

"Godsdamn," Gustavs said.

Anna stepped inside and, for lack of any better option, they followed her. Even Pūka. The damned cat stayed close to their feet, purring as the maalkonis sealed the tunnel behind them.

III

A ceaseless din filled the tunnel as Anna's atstru-torch emitted its golden light. Anna was right; this torch was much stronger. The maalkonis swirled a deep, inky black around the three of them—and Pūka—with flecks of violet, like dust on the wind. Justīne put a hand on the dirt wall beside her and listened in silence. Ievan and his supporters had found the tunnel. She could hear their footsteps plain as day, though the maalkonis obscured their view completely.

"You don't think they went in there?" a woman asked, catching her breath.

"Their footprints do," another man said. The sound of dirt sliding against metal. "Somebody brought a shovel and dug this out on purpose."

"Hells," the woman said.

"Pity," Ievan said. "Why would Ešlija fight for them so hard if they were only going to commit suicide?"

"Maybe they thought that we were going to kill them and wanted to die on their own terms. I told you that you should have left the arquebuses at the guardhouse, you idiots. Probably scared them into this."

Justīne glanced over at Gustavs. A tear descended across his cheek, and he was still as the grave. She put a hand on his, and Anna joined in with her free hand. His shaking lessened as he gripped their hands back.

"Ievan, what are you doing?" the woman asked, anxious.

"It doesn't make any sense," he said.

"Put the gun down. You've already used up a ton of balls and powder."

Gustavs wrapped an arm around her and Anna and shoved down, forcing them to the ground. A moment later, he fell flat on his stomach as well.

"Stop," the woman chided him still. "Firing into the maalkonis will be as effective as spreading a poultice on a corpse."

A man laughed at that. Then he said, "Let's just group up with the others, make sure they're alright. Not worth wasting our time here."

A moment passed before Ievan responded. "You're right," he said, and soon their voices faded away.

The three of them laid on the ground in silence for several long minutes after Ievan left the mouth of the tunnel. Pūka decided when they were finished as she began to mew and pace around them, sniffing the air. Justīne stood and brushed the dirt off of her chest and knees.

"They think we're dead," Gustavs said, his voice sounding distant.

"Probably best that way," Justīne said, finally fastening Niklāvs' sword to her belt. The weight felt odd but not uncomfortable. "We can figure out what to do next then take them by surprise, like Anna said."

"What is this place?" Gustavs asked. He looked around, keeping a hand on his sword.

"We don't really know," Anna admitted. She began walking deeper into the tunnel. The rest of them stayed close, not wanting to approach the edge of the sanctuary her torch created.

"We found this place two years ago," Justīne said, whispering. "Anna practically dragged me in, and we explored the tunnels."

"I guess some things don't change," Gustavs said.

"June's never been hard to convince." Anna shrugged. "And there was no way I was coming in here alone."

"What did you find in here? Does anyone else know about this or what that *torch* can do?"

"Dādi has some idea about the torch. He made the original one, but its 'failure' discouraged him from spending too much time on it. His attention has been on the atstrumeters and copper torches. Fixing stuff."

"Why?" Gustavs asked. "Why would you prevent him from working on an invention that allows us to traverse the dark? Monika and the mages before her worked at this for their entire lives."

"Because it's not safe here," Justīne whispered. "There are *things* in the dark."

Gustavs stopped walking. Matching her volume, he asked, "What exactly are we walking into right now?"

Anna shrugged. "Like I said, we don't really know."

"There's some evidence of human activity in here," Justīne added. "Brick structures and doors, and these tunnels are not natural. They're constructed like a labyrinth."

"Gustavs doesn't care about the *architecture*," Anna said. "Something lives down here. It's tall, quick, and has glowing purple eyes."

"Like the wisps," Gustavs said, glancing at the maalkonis around them.

Justīne nodded. "Yeah. We didn't get a good look at it last time, but we saw enough. And then it chased us out. It's where the scar on my back came from."

Gustavs grimaced. "I thought that was from some accident on the farm."

"Yeah… I lied about that."

"Hm. Should we turn back? Ievan and his people already think we're dead. We could leave right now, and they won't be looking for us."

Justīne said, "If Ievan and his crew made it up the hill, that means they broke through the line by the farmhouse. They may have the whole town by now. You saw the fires."

Anna nodded. "Ievan said they were outnumbered, but they attacked in the early hours of first dim, before everyone was awake. Caught us off-guard. We'll just be walking into that mess—a guard, a farmer, and an engineer. I don't like those odds."

"So, what?" Gustavs growled. "You want to give up? Wander the tunnels until the purple-eyed creature devours us?"

"Something out here has survived the maalkonis," Anna said wistfully.

"What are you planning?" Justīne asked.

"Our options right now are either walk into town, where I *know* there's at least a few dozen people who want to capture or kill us. Or we can explore these tunnels, where things aren't so clear-cut. Maybe it's a mistake. Or maybe we'll find something we can use. A weapon or something."

"And if we don't?" Gustavs asked.

Anna shrugged. "Then we go home all the same. Just a bit later in the day."

Gustavs stared at them both in turn.

"I don't like it either," Justīne said. "But it makes some sense. If we're quiet, we might not attract that creature—or anything else. If there's anything else. Just keep track of where we go, so we can get back. We outran that thing when we were kids, so we can probably do it again, but if we get lost, I don't want to imagine what would happen next."

Gustavs took a deep breath. "Fine. But we *don't* spend noctis in here. That's when the maalkonis is most active. If something's lurking out there, we need to stay alert."

Justīne nodded. "Of course. Anna, if we decide to go, we have to go."

"We'll cross that bridge when we get there," Anna said.

They turned left at the brick wall and right at the end of that path, following the same route that she and Anna had taken last time. Soon enough, they returned to the third fork and the door that lay between two branching paths. It was just as Justīne remembered. The door was made of old and heavy wood, slightly burnt along the edges and affixed on large rusty hinges. Anna tried the door's handle. It rattled in its hinges but did not budge.

"Hold this," Anna said, handing Justīne the atstru-torch. "Don't release this trigger. The light will go out, and you'll kill us all if you do."

"Oh, good," Justīne said, putting the torch into a death-grip.

Anna knelt in front of the door and withdrew a pair of thin, iron rods from her pocket, inserting them into a lock in the door.

"Do you need some light?" Justīne asked, holding the torch a bit higher.

"Not really. It's more about *feeling*."

"What are you doing?" Gustavs asked.

"This," Anna said, twisting one of the rods and giving the door a push.

It swung on creaky hinges as the torch's light banished the maalkonis from inside. A room, not unlike the ones

Justīne grew up in, lingered inside. It was small, with a hard cot in one corner and an empty washbasin in another. A bookshelf lay along one brick wall, half-filled. Some of the books had torn and fallen to the floor. A low table stood in the center of the room, its surface littered in dust, one of its legs broken in half. One corner of the tabletop was stained brown and black. Justīne carried the torch inside and held it up to the dark black marks.

"I didn't know you could pick locks," Gustavs whispered.

"This is incredible," Anna said, ignoring him.

"What do you think it is?" Justīne asked, nodding at the broken and filthy table.

"That's an old bloodstain," Gustavs said. "Probably from a fight. It's scattered, chaotic. Every now and then, the guards use sharpened steel and duel until somebody bleeds. They get bored. The blood they leave on the ground looks a lot like this—but never this much."

"The black is… Ink?" Anna added, questioningly. Then, with more confidence, she added, "It was drawn in patterns, purposeful. These lines and circles are too precise. They might be runes. I think I recognize this one."

"Gods." Gustavs groaned. "Don't tell me there's a mage wandering around here."

"Probably a carving from before the maalkonis," Justīne said. "It took a long time for the darkness to advance this far. Regular people lived out here once. Does that rune mean anything?"

"I'm not sure," Anna said. "Well, yes, it means *something*, but the runes all look so similar. I think Monika described it as 'wind' or 'gust,' something like that. I don't recognize the others at all though. Maybe the fight this mage got into damaged the writing. Or she wrote the wrong rune, and *it* caused this damage."

"Well, they were writing directly onto the table, so things probably weren't going well to start with."

"Wait," Gustavs said. "Anna, you've been learning to write runes?"

She smiled innocently. "I think they're neat. What can I say?"

Gustavs laughed, though his eyes looked panicked.

"Look," Anna continued. "I think those books are important. Even if I never use them to their potential—and I've never *written* a rune before; I just try to understand them—I think *somebody* in The Old Town should have a sense for them. The arcane is strong, and we may need it one day."

Something clattered off the bookshelf—out of the corner of her eye Justīne caught the flutter of a book falling. She spun. Pūka stared back at her from one of the shelves, one paw raised, a book on the ground.

"Godsdamned cat," she muttered. Then, in the dark of the maalkonis, in the hall they'd come from, she swore that she saw a flash of violet light. She put her hand on the grip of Niklāvs' sword. "Did either of you see that?" she whispered.

"Something out there?" Gustavs asked, keeping his voice low as well.

They waited a moment, the sound of the torch filling the room. It was awfully hard to be quiet with that thing whirring. But the violet light never came back. Perhaps she was just working herself up.

Justīne handed the torch back to Anna. "Let's keep moving," she said.

Anna nodded. Then, quietly, "Let's try to come back through here on the way out. I'd love to look through that bookshelf Pūka found. Maybe we could bring some of them back with us."

"We'll see," Gustavs said.

It was probably near midday when they encountered a bridge. It was made of wood, supported by rope and rusty nails, and suspended over a wide chasm. A well of deep black churned in its basin. Justīne felt a tightness in her chest as she stared down into the void. As Anna approached with her torch, it revealed slightly more—walls of rock with paltry, singed vines that still clung to it. Still, the maalkonis seemed to compress down there into something even darker. There were several stories about how the apocalyptic clouds came about, none agreeing with each other. Justīne supposed the idea that it arose from such pits wasn't too far out of the ordinary, though it was impossible to tell if that were the truth, and she had no desire to find out.

Gustavs tested the bridge, gingerly placing a foot on one of its planks. It shook under his boot, and a sheen of dust fell from the planks

"This place is *malsavekzīme*," Justīne said.

Anna said, "The line between good and bad luck is thin. *Malsavekzīme* and *lavekzīme* are two sides of the same coin, and it's easy to mistake one for the other. Let's keep moving and figure out which Luck has offered us."

Gustavs shook his head at the bridge. "Malsavekzīme. I'd wager my sword that thing will collapse if we try to cross. Luck is playing tricks on us."

A shrill quiet voice arose from the maalkonis like a whispered prayer. Justīne looked for the violet eyes but saw nothing in the dark.

"The Hells was that?" Gustavs wondered aloud.

Justīne whispered, "It could be one of those creatures—the thing that lives in the maalkonis. I think we were spotted back in the empty room. Remember, I thought I saw something, but it had vanished when you both turned to look."

Gustavs loosed a long sigh. "We go one at a time, then. If the ropes snap, no sense in all three of us…" He trailed off, but Justīne knew how that sentence was supposed to end. There was no sense in all three of them dying. "Keep your legs spread wide," Gustavs continued. "The boards are old and rotting, I think you want to keep your weight spread out. I'll go first."

"We could keep looking around for a safer path."

"We could. You want to wander around some more or put this chasm between us and whatever's making that noise behind us?" Gustavs asked.

When neither of them responded, he put his hands on the rope railings. "I'll go first," he said, his hands shaking.

Gustavs steadied himself with a slow breath. Then he took his first step onto the bridge. It swayed under his weight but did not break. Another step, and the wooden board creaked, but again it did not break.

"You can do this," Anna said softly.

Gustavs did not respond. Justīne could see the muscles in his arms tense as he pressed down onto the rope railings, offsetting some of his weight onto them. He stepped forward again, and the plank snapped in half, his foot shooting through the rotten wood.

Justīne heard a shout escape both hers and Anna's mouths.

Gustavs clung to the ropes for a moment then pulled himself back up and found his footing on the next plank. It held, mercifully.

Somewhere in the distance, the creature in the maalkonis chittered at them. It sounded closer. She glanced at Anna, who looked a bit less confident about this adventure than she had been. Justīne felt the same uncertainty clawing at her chest, threatening to over-whelm her. But surely nothing better awaited them back in The Old Town. They could run, but they would have achieved practically nothing. Justīne hated every second of this nightmare, but they had already come so far. Even if they couldn't find a way to save the Ļaodil, seeing the books and runes in that room they'd passed through earlier gave Justīne a measure of hope. Perhaps there were some answers about this place tucked away out in the dark. If they could just survive the journey through this wretched place.

Pūka had apparently decided that she had waited long enough and followed Gustavs across. He muttered as the cat waltzed past him with ease and made it to the other side. Pūka sat down on the opposite ledge, curled her tail over her paws, and watched Gustavs stumble after her.

"I don't like your cat, Justīne," he yelled back at her.

Justīne smiled. "Get in line."

"Poor Pūka." Anna chuckled. "How could either of you be mad at that little face?"

Gustavs reached the other side of the chasm after another minute. The torch's light barely encompassing him and Pūka. They stood at the edge of its sanctuary, the maalkonis reaching toward them with fibrous, inky tendrils.

Anna went next, copying Gustavs' technique as best as she could while still holding the torch. The light and the maalkonis wavered as much as the rickety bridge. Anna placed her feet slowly, carefully, avoiding the worst of the rot as much as she could. She made it halfway across the bridge when her legs began to shake, and one foot burst through the boards. Justīne felt her heart drop as she watched splinters and mold fall into the chasm below.

"Throw me the torch," Gustavs told her.

"I… I can't."

"If you lose your balance, we're *all* done. Throw it to me so you can focus on getting across."

Anna steadied herself as best she could and took another step. The bridge shook as she shifted her weight, and she nearly fell.

"Anna!" Gustavs and Justīne both shouted.

The creature in the maalkonis chittered again. When Justīne looked over her shoulder, she swore that she saw its eyes flashing at her. In a blink, they were gone. She cursed and noticed the sweat forming along her back. This was taking too long.

"I can't!" Anna said. "If I let go of the trigger, the light will go out."

"I'll come to you, then," Gustavs said.

Gustavs stepped onto the bridge, and it wobbled under his weight. His face was stoic and severe, but sweat formed on his brow and his breathing became strained. Justīne wished she could do more to help, but she worried that adding her own weight to the bridge as well would cause it to weaken even more, or her own unsure footing would make it more difficult for her siblings to get across.

Anna passed the torch to Gustavs, and the maalkonis lurched toward Justīne. He walked back first, and the light's sanctuary moved away with him. A sheer wall of darkness rolled toward her, ravenous and ceaseless. On instinct, she drew Niklāvs' sword and backed toward the ledge, bracing herself to fight Death itself.

"Made it!" Gustavs shouted.

The wall of darkness had stopped no more than a meter from Justīne, but the blade had been enveloped by it. She pulled it out of the dark quickly, but it came away changed. The tip of the sword had turned a silver color. Cracks along the steel glowed violet. At her touch, a shard fell, leaving her with a shorter blade and a tip like a sewing needle. She wanted to swear and curse the Gods, but that wouldn't have helped. All that she had left of Niklāvs was ruined.

"June," Anna called to her.

Her sister had made it to the other side as well. Gustavs had handed the torch back to her, and they both stood at the center of its light. It was her turn to cross.

She would have to worry about the sword later. Justīne sheathed it carefully and took a deep breath. She could almost feel the maalkonis at her back, reaching for her, eager to tear her apart. She tried to focus instead on the sound of the torch's whirring and took her first step.

Wooden planks creaked under her feet, but she offset her weight with the rope railings. They groaned and wavered but did not snap. She reminded herself that she was lighter than Gustavs, and he'd made it across safely, so she should be alright too. Unless the bridge had become weaker by his and Anna's crossing.

She took another step, avoiding a spot where the rotten planks had broken during her siblings' crossings. She took another step, feeling the bridge shudder under her hands and feet. Another step, and the wood underfoot broke. She pulled her leg back up quickly, scraping it against the bridge. Beads of crimson welled up on her knee, through her trousers.

"Hells. Are you okay?" Gustavs asked.

Justīne looked up at her siblings and nodded. They were probably twenty paces away still. She could make it. She had to. "Just a sliver."

Somewhere in the distance, the creature in the maalkonis gave a shrill cry. Gods, it sounded close. When Justīne glanced back at where she'd come from, she saw its violet eyes bearing down at her through the dark.

"It won't come into the light," Anna said, her voice shaky. "This torch is stronger than the last one, and it's got a full charge. Just keep moving, June."

She took another step, and the creature behind her wailed. Something akin to words filled the air, like a chant. Justīne chanced a look over her shoulder and saw the thing's arm breach the barrier that Anna's torch created. Its hand, with fingers black as soot and claws for nails, reached toward them, jagged veins of violet shooting across its pale white skin—like the cracks in Niklāvs' sword. Spikes and black feathers sprouted from it, a mess of shapes which made the arm look like a broken wing, and black blood dripped toward its elbow.

"Run!" Anna shouted at her. "Forget what I said. *Run!*"

Justīne sprinted across the rest of the bridge, feeling wood splinter and break under her boots. As she reached the edge, the planks finally gave way, and she fell. Justīne felt her heart leap into her throat. She reached out toward the ledge, scrambling, digging her fingers into whatever she could. The rock scraped her hands and arms, cutting into her skin. She could feel herself slipping.

Anna and Gustavs each took one of Justīne's hands and pulled her up. They leaned back, using their own weight to help lift her, and Justīne stumbled over the ledge.

Then, in the same fluid motion, Gustavs let go of her and drew his blade. He struck one of the bridge's rope railings and it collapsed entirely, the remaining rotten planks no longer suspended on one side. They dangled from the other end, rattling against each other.

The creature was nowhere to be seen. Only dirt and darkness surrounded them.

"Did that thing fall?" Justīne asked.

"No," Gustavs said. "It never quite got into the light. But now it shouldn't be able to follow us. I hope."

"How will we get back?" Justīne asked, trying to quell the quivering in her voice.

"Don't worry," Anna said. "We will find a way. There's always a way."

The maalkonis roiled above them as they left the tunnels. The sun was little more than a dim speck in the sky, casting a meek light over everything. It looked as though it was already last dim—though that was certainly better than the pitch black of the tunnels. A part of Justīne was surprised that the sun touched anything beyond The Old Town at all.

Pūka walked ahead of them as they stepped into a field of rolling hills. What looked like irrigation ditches clung to the land, and dead grassy stalks still stood in neat rows. Justīne imagined that this might have once been farmland long ago. When she touched one of the blackened plants, it crumbled to ash at her touch. She shook and rubbed her hands together to get it off, but black marks remained as if she'd been holding charcoal.

They traveled in silence for some time. Justīne wondered if any other creatures lurked in the dark, or if the one they'd left behind would be able to find them. She found herself looking over her shoulder frequently and caught Gustavs doing the same. She smiled at him, acknowledging their shared discomfort with this place. He stared back at her—no, his eyes were focused on something in the distance. She looked in the same direction just as Anna pointed out the dark shape on the hill ahead of them.

"What is that?" Anna wondered at a tall dark shape with a tower jutting out from its center, only visible by the thin and partially obscured streaks of violet light that came from it.

Gustavs said, "Let's stick to the fields. If we keep our distance, we should keep out of the way of whatever's there."

Anna shook her head. "No, we should go see what's there. If we're to find anything of use in the maalkonis, my bet's on the glowing purple tower, not the barren fields."

Justīne sighed. "She's got a point."

"That could be the creature's home, or its nest," Gustavs said.

"We left that thing behind us."

"There could be more. Or there could be other paths to get here. We don't really know anything."

"True." Anna shrugged. "We'll be quiet. In and out before anyone or anything notices."

Anna walked in the direction of the tower, Pūka at her heels. Justīne and Gustavs begrudgingly followed her, staying close to Anna in the atstru-torch's light. If she were honest with herself, Justīne *was* curious about the dark tower. However, with every step toward it, she fought a terror building inside her, roiling as angrily as the maalkonis itself.

"You're going to get us all killed," Gustavs hissed at Anna.

"Don't bother," Justīne said. She felt her heart pounding again. She tried to control her breathing. "Once Anna gets an idea in her head, you can't talk her out of it. Besides, I *do* want to see what's here."

"What if I just refuse?" Gustavs crossed his arms and stood his ground. Justīne and Anna stopped so as not to let him leave the torch's light. He continued, "You said you wanted to come in here to escape the fighting, but now we're in the middle of the maalkonis, without a clear path home, and something is following us. Hunting us, probably."

"You're the one who cut the rope on that bridge," Anna said.

"To save you both," he said, exasperated and exhausted in equal measure. "Whatever that thing was, I don't know if I could have stopped it if it broke through the torch's light."

"Look," Justīne said, "We're this far. The tower is right there. Let's go check it out, and then we can start looking for a way back."

"Maybe we can go over the tunnels," Anna suggested. "When we left, I think I saw some rocks we could climb near where we exited. I'll bet we could find a way to climb over the north wall once we reach it. Or we can walk around and look for the gate by the river."

Gustavs nodded. "Fine. But after this, no more adventures. We're not stopping in any more abandoned places, and we're *not* going back in the tunnels. We march directly over them, back to The Old Town. I can fight Ievan and the rest if I have to, but the maalkonis…"

"Sure," Justīne said, agreeing before Anna could respond. "One more stop, then we go back."

Gustavs huffed. He glanced up at the tower in front of them. "This is a mistake. Please don't touch anything that looks like it might kill you. And don't touch the tower either. I don't trust anything that glows purple."

"Yes, sir," Anna grumbled at him with a mock salute.

Anna began to walk in the direction of the tower. Justīne and Gustavs followed closely. Gustavs shot her a look. She'd never seen him so anxious. She understood it, but somehow she didn't feel all that nervous. Mostly, she felt numb. She was certain that the insanity of this day would hit her later, but for now, it was all she could do to put one foot in front of the other.

The fields gave way to stone and rubble as they ascended the hill. The dark mass at the top turned out to be an old brick building; the tower was actually a massive tree growing out of the structure's center. It had long since erupted through the ceiling and shattered the rafters. An old farmhouse, perhaps, considering the fields? That didn't explain the tree inside of it, but the place also looked far too small and isolated to be anything else.

The building was rather small, its rafters were rotted and broken along the ground, grey and red mushrooms sprouting out of the wood. Justīne had to raise her knees high to step over them. One of the building's walls had come down as well, casting wood and bricks around the area. A wind came through, rattling what remained of the old house and shaking the tree's immense branches.

A shallow pool had formed in the center of the building, beside the tree. The water was murky with rust and rot. Justīne realized how thirsty she was, but she resisted the urge to cup her hands and drink from it, despite the way her throat ached for relief. She'd rather be thirsty than sick. Gustavs' warnings resonated in her head.

Filthy as the pool was, its water was so still that it reflected her image back at her. Justīne touched her face, which had apparently become covered in dirt and grime. Soot, perhaps. Where her fingers trailed, the charcoal-like substance from those damned stalks trailed across her cheek. She did her best to wipe her face clean, but without using any pool water, there wasn't much to be done.

The massive tree appeared to be some kind of oak, and stood at least three times the height of the building it grew out of, probably taller than the old cathedral. It was hard to tell, exactly, given the way its form blurred into the maalkonis. Dim violet cracks showed through its bark, not unlike the way Niklāvs' sword had been damaged. However, now that Justīne was close, she was stunned to find dark green leaves and otherwise healthy bark on it. The monstrous tree had survived the maalkonis. In fact, it seemed to be thriving. When she touched a leaf, a shock of violet raced away from it, up through the cracks in the bark and ascending toward the sky, out of sight. She jolted backward, accidentally plucking the load from its branch.

"Careful," Gustavs warned. "I said no touching purple shit. We don't know what that thing is or how the maalkonis has affected it."

"It's just remarkable that it's alive," Justīne said. "I thought that *everything* died out here. So far, aside from that creature that was following us, everything has been dead. I wonder what makes this tree special."

"I haven't a clue," Anna said, looking closer at a leaf. Its edges were singed, like so many other things in the maalkonis, but the rest of it looked healthy. A thin wax coated the center of the leaf, smooth between her fingers.

Anna moved the torch up to its bark, peering closer at the violet trails that ran through it. Sap leaked from the fissures like bleeding wounds, trickling down into the soil and the water around it. Justīne noticed more green plants around the pool, which seemed to spread throughout the still water like a plague. Some were recognizable as mosses, others were completely submerged, and at first, they resembled something more akin to green milk that had been accidentally spilled into the pool. She didn't have a word for what that could possibly be. She wondered if it was something new or if it was a plant that only existed outside of The Old Town. Perhaps the maalkonis had created it, or it had some natural resistance, like the oak.

Anna moved on, occupying herself near the tallest wall. After a few moments, she said, "Look at this."

Anna held the torch beside a small collection of books that she found on a desk behind her, neatly stacked under a pile of rubble. She picked one from the stack. It was a haggard old thing, stained by dirt and water damage. Whoever wrote it appeared to have done so carefully, with a practiced hand and clean lines of ink. Diagrams were drawn on some pages.

Justīne recognized arcane runes similar to those from Monika's books, but she didn't know what any of them meant. They were drawn in halves to avoid actually casting a spell, with a divider separating each rune's left and right side. It appeared as if the author of the book took the time to write down some notes about each one—if not define the illustrations. Most were accompanied by long descriptions or results from some trials.

"This is incredible," Anna said. "This isn't quite like Monika's books. It's certainly not her handwriting."

"How is it different?" Justīne asked.

"It's less of a guide book, more of a… It's like a workbook. It's explaining things sporadically. The author was jotting notes down, results from tests, working on something. I think they were trying to find the right rune, or maybe even create their own. I don't know if a mage *can* create runes. Monika theorized that there might be runes she didn't know about, but she never mentions *creating* one."

"Why would somebody need to create a rune?"

"And why would that person leave their notes in the maalkonis?" Gustavs added.

"I don't know," Anna said. "But I… Look, some of these runes match the ones on that table in the tunnels. I was right. This one is labeled 'gust of wind,' and I remember seeing this one, it's labelled 'sunder.' This might be the same person. But they're both crossed out, like somebody made a mistake writing them."

A moment of silence passed between them. Then Gustavs asked, "Runes are kind of like commands, right? The words they represent force change upon the world."

"Kind of," Anna said, still flipping through the book. "They summon things into the world, like the *concept* of something. For example, 'gust' is less about a literal gust and more the idea of a sudden rush of wind. Quick and wild movements of the air. The word 'gust' is just the best description of—"

"My point is," Gustavs interrupted her, "all of those words are about pushing something away or destroying it. And before the maalkonis, mages fought in wars. Weaponized their runes."

"No wars anymore. At least, I don't think anyone in the maalkonis would be in one."

"So, not a war mage," Justīne said. "But Gustavs is right. What if this mage was trying to get rid of the maalkonis? Gust, sunder, ways to push it away or destroy the darkness. They were testing something, trying to find the right rune to cast a—I assume—powerful spell. Something they had ideas for but couldn't quite figure out."

"Maybe," Anna said. As she flipped through the pages, the writing became more rushed, the descriptions shorter, and the runes' linework less exact. Anna stopped on a page entirely made up of large foreign runes and blood stains mixed in with the dried ink. "Doesn't seem to have worked out very well."

"Do you think they practiced blood magic? I've heard Dādi talk about how some people once turned to that as a last-ditch effort to stop the maalkonis. Before we figured out how to build the atstrumeters," Justīne said.

"I don't think so," Anna said, flipping back to the front of the book.

"Blood magic never worked," Gustavs said. His hand was firmly on his sword, ready to draw in a moment's notice. "Mama told me once that The Old Town outlawed it even before the gate closed for the final time."

"He's right. Monika was very clear about that in her books," Anna said. She flipped through the pages, adding, "There is blood on these pages, but it looks more like whoever wrote this was wounded. They bled on their work rather than painting the runes with their blood. It's not a part of the runes; it looks like an accident. Also, look at how faded the writing is here in the beginning. It's older. Here in the back"—she flipped to the back of the book and in a whisper said—"it hasn't faded hardly at all. I'd wager to say that it's *fresh*."

Justīne felt a shiver run up her spine. "Ink takes a while to fade."

"So maybe the final pages weren't written yesterday, but somebody had been working on this recently, and they've been working on it for years. I think there's somebody else out here, and they've been trying to figure out… Some kind of problem. I'll need more time to find out what they were trying to do. It'll be easier when I can look at Monika's books as well, once we get back to town. I don't recognize most of these runes or what they're supposed to do, though. I also wonder why whoever wrote this would just leave it behind. Were they expecting to come back, or hiding it from somebody, or simply finishing it?"

Justīne looked down at the makeshift cubby she'd found the books in. It did seem as though somebody had made a place for them. She wished she had some answers for Anna.

"I'll hold onto it for you if you want," was all she could offer, "so you can hold on to the torch."

Anna closed the book and handed it to her, moving onto the next. "It's hard to say anything for sure now, but this… This might be worth all the trouble of coming out here. We might finally be able to get some answers, maybe even train a new mage for The Old Town."

Justīne understood that the books might be important, but the oak tree and the smaller plants around its base were what drew her in. Among them were a couple of daisies and a blueberry bush. They were small, probably lacking enough nutrition and light to grow properly, but they were alive. One of the daisies was budding, trying to form a bright white flower, and a few blueberries had formed along the bush. Most were small and green, but one was nearly ripe, a rosy purple color. She picked it. The berry snapped away from the bush easily, the brittle stem breaking at the slightest pressure, but none of it crumbled to ash. In fact, the berry seemed fresh and ripe. Was the tree keeping it alive? Or perhaps the building had some kind of arcane protection?

"I thought we agreed not to touch things that could kill us," Gustavs said, weariness in his voice.

"Right," she said. Her curiosity soured, and she flicked the blueberry into the pool. Ripples spread across the water's surface, bouncing off one another. The tree's dim reflection wavered in the water.

"Wait," Gustavs said, peering into the water where Justīne had tossed the berry.

Justīne looked with him, but it was too dark to make anything out other than the rust, wood, and green slime. Anna drew closer and held the torch over the water. It reflected the light back at them, and the water rippled.

She moved the torch, and the ripples seemed to move with it.

"That's odd," Gustavs said, a deep crinkle in the middle of his brow.

That was when Justīne noticed the shape underneath the water. In the light, the way Anna was holding it, she could see that there was something beneath the surface. A white, clawed hand emerged from the pool. Its nails were long, sharp, and black. Violet veins of light ran up the arm, then the creature's head emerged, and it swiveled quickly, locking its violet eyes with hers.

Justīne leapt back, drew Niklāvs' sword, and pushed Anna aside. She heard her sister stumble. For a moment, the torch's light flickered, and the maalkonis pulsated hungrily, threatening to lunge at them from all sides.

Gustavs had also drawn his blade and adopted a defensive stance. Justīne copied it as best she could. She kept the sword low and bent her knees. The muscles in her legs were taught, ready should she need to dodge the white creature's claws or lunge forward to cut it down.

The creature lurched up from the pool, water dripping down its arms, shoulders, and black hair so long that the ends were still submerged. Seeing it so close and in the light, Justīne noticed the creature had the shape of a woman and wore tattered rags over her body, though her silhouette seemed to be tearing it-self apart. Feathers black as noctis hung off their arms, chest, and face—one that had no mouth—hanging off their pallid, nearly-white skin, with new pin feathers budding around the existing ones. Bone spurs also jutted out through the skin, all across her body. Where they protruded, beads of black blood appeared around them, mixing with the water and dripping shades of grey. Now, Justīne could see that the violet fissures were also on the woman's legs and neck, and they all reached toward her heart. Or where Justīne assumed her heart would be.

In that instant, Justīne was sure that this was the same creature which had pursued them by the bridge. The arm that reached through the torch's light, which looked like a broken wing, was the same.

The woman turned her head up toward the sky silent-ly, eyes wide open. It almost looked like she was prac-ticing some ancient prayer, standing there with water dripping off of her claws and down her chin. Justīne offered the Gods a prayer of her own, though she wasn't sure if they could hear anyone out in the dark, or if they ever listened to anyone. How could they possibly be here, about to die at the hands of this creature, if the Gods were watching over them?

Pūka broke the silence. She leapt on one of the boughs of the oak tree, hissing at the woman in the pool. Justīne tried to shoo the cat away, but the feathered woman moved first. Her claws reached behind her, seeming to move before the rest of her body, then she spun and contorted as she struck at the cat. Pūka kept her distance. She leapt to another branch, then another, ascending the tree.

"Why isn't the torch stopping it?" Gustavs asked.

"I don't know," Anna said, pointing it at the woman. "Maybe because she appeared already inside of it?"

Nothing happened.

"Turn it off," Justīne said.

"What?" Anna shrieked.

Justīne stepped closer to Anna and Gustavs, keeping the sword between her and the feathered woman. "Remember the bridge? The light held her back, but only while she was in the dark. It was like a wall, but she's on our side of the wall this time. Turn it off, return her to darkness, then turn it back on again before the maalkonis reaches us."

"I don't like that," Gustavs said. "You've seen how quickly the maalkonis fills in whatever the torch's light doesn't reach. If we don't time it exactly right—"

"And what about Pūka?" Anna asked.

The feathered woman's glare found them as it lost interest in Pūka. Or perhaps the cat had ascended beyond the feathered woman's reach. The woman stared violet daggers at them, watching like an owl might track mice as they moved through the grass. She cocked her head and a clicking sound emitted from her, echoing off the ruined building's walls.

"Do it," Gustavs said, stepping close to her and Anna.

"Okay," Anna said. "If this doesn't go well—"

The woman stepped back on one foot, spine hunched and feathers raised, and extended her long claws. In the same moment, Gustavs moved between the woman and them, his sword pointed in the creature's direction.

"Do it!" he shouted.

The light flicked off, and the world returned to darkness. The torch's gears stopped, leaving an eerie silence in their wake. The dim light of the sun was all that remained, but it was still so dark that Justīne couldn't see the sword in her own hands, let alone her siblings at her side. She could feel them pressing against her back, and she could hear their ragged breaths. Their presence gave her strength, even as the inky black tore toward them, no longer hindered by the torch. If she was to die here, at least she wouldn't be alone.

However, she could see the shape of the great oak, thanks to its violet veins, the reflection of it off the pool, and the same violet cracks in the feathered woman's body. Hers were a blur as she leapt in the air, and as the maalkonis raced toward them, it began to obscure the violet light.

An audible click filled the ruined building as Anna flicked the torch back on. Its light repelled the maalkonis, and the torch's gears began to spin again. The woman, as if struck by a great hammer, was propelled against one of the building's walls. Bricks collapsed from it and fell where she'd landed just beyond the torch's light.

Gustavs ran to the edge of the light and shouted for Anna to follow him. She stepped forward a few paces, enough for the light to fall across the feathered woman's body. Gustavs raised his sword as the woman glared up at him, her skin singed and her body bleeding black. She caught Gustavs' arm as he swung, her claws digging into his muscle. Justīne ran forward, but by the time she arrived, he'd wrenched himself free.

The woman attempted to stand, and Justīne swung. The feathered woman grabbed the blade, and it dug into her palm, black blood filling the gaps between her fingers and catching in her feathers. She pushed against

Justīne as Gustavs drove his blade into her chest. The strength in the woman's arm vanished, and her violet gaze faltered. She fell there in the rubble of the old building.

"Are you hurt?" Justīne asked Gustavs.

She put down Niklāvs' sword and took his wounded arm. It was bleeding from where the woman had clawed him. It was difficult to tell just how deep the cuts were.

"Pūka," Anna called for the cat.

"It could be worse." Gustavs winced.

"Hold on," Justīne said and ripped a strip of cloth from the bottom of her tunic. It wasn't the cleanest bandage, and the cold air chilled her skin, but it was all she had. Her cloak would keep her warm. Justīne wrapped his arm in the rag, tying it tightly around his wounds.

"Ouch," he complained as she knotted it.

"You'll get over it," Justīne teased. Blood was already staining the cloth, but at least it wasn't dripping all over his arm anymore. "Tell me if it starts to feel weird. Numb. Anything like that. If we make it out of here, you'll want to wash it with fresh water and get yourself a better bandage. I'm sure Sofija could help you more."

"This is perfect. Thank you."

"I can't find Pūka," Anna said.

She'd wandered over to the tree, looking up into its branches. Justīne joined her, resisting the urge to wash Gustavs' blood off in the pool. She wiped it on her tunic—it was ruined now anyway—and called for the cat. Violet eyes appeared from the tree's branches.

"Shit," she hissed and ran to get Niklāvs' sword. Gustavs had already picked it up. He handed it to her. When Justīne finally turned around, the violet eyes were already gone. "Where did it go?"

The eyes reappeared, then disappeared. When Justīne saw them again, the creature had moved somewhere else in the tree's branches. It was silent as it descended, approaching them. Then, at the edge of the darkness, Pūka appeared. Her rusty red coat was singed, the fur around her eyes black as noctis and her irises a glowing violet.

"Pūka, I'm sorry," Anna whispered. Tears welled up in the corner of her eyes.

"This cat is still here," Pūka said.

Her voice seemed to echo around the ruined building as if multiple speakers intoned each word. The cat's voice cracked like an unpracticed singer, yet she exuded confidence. Justīne swore when she heard purring through the words even as the maalkonis tugged at Pūka's fur and she breathed in the inky blackness.

"What?" Anna asked, taking a step away from Pūka.

"This cat is here," the voice came again. She took a step forward. "I am sorry… Frightening and… Fighting you three. It has been… It has been *ages* since I saw another person. Certainly since I saw one who was not cursed. But the darkness muddles the mind, and you all drew steel. Fire. You have ventured so far…" The cat's words were strained, but a twinkle shone in her shining, violet eyes, and her whiskers twitched. Was Pūka *grinning* at them?

"How are you talking?" Gustavs asked.

"All things in the maalkonis are bonded," she said as if that explained everything. "Put my body back into the water. I will explain as best I can."

"You're the woman with the feathers," Justīne said.

The cat blinked at them. "Yes."

"No," Gustavs said. "I'm sorry, but Graudiņš' cat is not—"

"That name…" The cat purred. "That name is familiar. An old life…" A long pause followed. Justīne got the sense that the cat—the woman—was no longer looking at them. Her eyes were unfocused and hazy. When it spoke again, its already-cracking voice became hoarse as well. "I see. The Old Town, of course. It's been so long. I forgot so much. A shame the old man has passed. He was a kind soul. Used to sneak me sweets when I was a girl. And you three… Children of Oḷegs."

Justīne gripped the sword. "How do you know all of this? How do you know our Dādi?"

"Pūka has offered her memories. She has seen much."

"How do you know The Old Town?"

"These books"—Anna took the book of runes from her and held it up—"did you write them? You're a mage?"

The cat purred again, bobbing its head. "The water," it said, its voice trembling. At the same time, its eyes pulsed violet.

Whatever connection the feathered woman and the cat shared was failing; Justīne was certain of it. They could just let that connection fade. The feathered woman was no longer a threat. They would be able to pack up and find a way back to The Old Town safely. Or as safely as one could. Once she died, they might be able to help Pūka somehow.

Anna set the book down and approached the feathered woman. "Come on."

"You can't be serious," Gustavs said.

"We already came all this way, and now we can talk to each other. I want answers."

The cat watched them intently from its perch on the tree's bough. Its voice croaked and clicked when it opened its mouth again, whiskers twitching.

"Hells with it," Justīne said and sheathed the sword. "Gustavs, are you still able to fight? If she attacks again, we end it for good."

He nodded. "This is a bad idea."

"Maybe," she agreed. "But Anna's right. We've already come this far, and we've proven that we can beat her."

Pūka blinked at her slowly, the tip of her tail twitching.

"Okay," Justīne said. "Let's hurry up, Anna."

She wasn't sure what the pool's water would do, but a lack of understanding was nothing new when it came to the maalkonis. She and Anna lifted the woman by her arms and legs. She tried not to think of how the woman's feathers brushed against her palms, or how she had to hold her by the forearms because her wrists were littered in bone spurs sharp as daggers. She tried not to think about how much pain the feathered woman must have been in. She hoped that the poor cat wasn't hurt too.

They threw the woman's body into the pool. Water splashed on the opposite side, spraying across the mosses and the ruinous floor. Gustavs kept his sword trained on the cat, his eyes darting between it and the water. Justīne drew her weapon as well and kept it between the pool and her sister.

The water began to still and, after a moment, the violet was gone from Pūka's eyes. Anna raised her torch higher and took a step closer to the pool. Justīne moved with her, peering into the murky water. Pūka watched from her perch as well, just beyond the protection of Anna's light.

The woman erupted from the pool, already within the protection of Anna's torch, her body lurching upward as if it were tied to a rope. She righted herself more quickly this time and took in her surroundings, the violent agitation that once filled her seemingly gone. Though there was still a wild, animal-like quality in her gaze. As the woman raised her hands, a violet light emitted from her blackened fingertips. They carved intricate patterns in the air, one of the arcane runes. Justīne adjusted her stance, ready to fight. But although the woman was casting some kind of spell, her movements were calm. They were quick with the kind of expertise one got from years of training, not as though she was rushing to attack them.

As her claws arced through the air one final time, a violet rune appeared on Pūka's forehead, and another arose on her throat. Before Justīne could react, the cat walked through the torch's sanctuary with ease. The maalkonis was not able to follow it inside. Rather, it seemed like some of the darkness, which had been caught in the cat's fur, evaporated away. It only lasted a moment, and the change was minimal, but Justīne was sure of what she saw.

"There," the woman said through Pūka's purring voice, which began to come through the cat's mouth more easily than before. Though the feathered woman's jaws worked, they did so silently as she still had no mouth to speak with. The rune on the cat's throat glowed as she spoke through the cat. "Together at last."

"You're not going to—" Gustavs started to ask.

"Did you write this?" Anna interrupted him, holding up the book she'd found.

The woman looked pointedly at Gustavs, and through Pūka she said, "Thank you for your help. I promise that I will try not to hurt anyone here. I do not want to fight… The light is helping to clear my mind." Then, turning to Anna, "I see you found some of my work."

"It *is* yours. I am not a mage, but from what I can tell, this is full of cleansing and banishment spells. What exactly were you working on?"

The woman took on a pained expression. "What does one do trapped in the dark but seek the light? I was trying to find my way home, and removing the maalkonis was the only way I thought I might be able to do that. Even if I could only remove a small part, just enough space to regain control of my own mind. As you've done for me here." She gestured at the sanctuary of light that Anna had created.

"What about Oļegs?" Gustavs asked. "You spoke as if you recognized his name."

The woman carved a line of violet light in the air with her long claws, forming another rune that turned into an image: a trio of shimmering stars. They seemed to move on their own for a moment before they fell away like sand in the wind.

"I knew him once. He is one of the few things about my old life that I can still remember sometimes. Most of my memories from before are like trying to catch ash in the wind."

Justīne let her hand drop from the sword. The pieces of this strange encounter began to fit together. According to Dādi, it had been several years since a woman had disappeared. So few people truly went *missing*. The Old Town wasn't a big place. A body was either found, or they at least discovered evidence of their walk into the maalkonis. To find somebody who could draw glimmers in the air…

"You're Karīna," she said, and in unison both the woman's and cat's heads snapped in her direction.

Karīna's expression softened. She appeared slightly rejuvenated, her pale skin almost radiant in the dark. Pūka purred on her behalf and said, "It has been *years* since I heard that name."

There wasn't much food to go around. Justīne had a piece of bread and some dried apple slices, and Anna had thought to bring part of a loaf of rye when she'd fled. They split the meager meal between the three of them. Anna offered some of hers to Karīna, but she refused, and Pūka had no appetite for such things. She knew that it helped, but Justīne felt hunger gnawing at her even more so after eating. She worried about the cat as well; Pūka hadn't eaten much at prausme, and who knew when Karīna's last meal was. Without a mouth, perhaps she simply didn't eat anymore. Or, like the cat, perhaps she had no appetite for anything they could offer. She hoped it was the former. A part of her still worried that their Dādi's old friend would somehow devour them, that this was all some ruse for her to get close. But since her resurrection, she'd been nothing but helpful. So far.

Gustavs led their repukdau prayer, offering his apologies to the Gods for failing to pray at prausme and imploring for their help. Justīne responded in kind, though her mind was elsewhere. Surely the Gods would understand. After all, they were sharing a meal in the maalkonis with a zombie mage and a talking cat. Nothing made sense anymore.

While they ate, Anna asked Karīna about the book she'd written and the symbols in it. The feathered woman responded through Pūka, clearly struggling to recall writing it. She spoke as if every word had to be unearthed and brushed of dirt.

"After I realized that the maalkonis wouldn't kill me, I tried to return to The Old Town, but it had formed a kind of wall that I could barely pierce—the edge of the darkness. I could reach into the light, but only for a moment. Walking back to The Old Town, leaving the maalkonis, those hopes died quickly. So, I tried to remember what I could of the runes my mother taught me and began to write them down. I hoped that I could make an opening to escape through, or carve out a space of my own. I didn't know why, but I could *feel* that I was in a race against time."

Justīne remembered the way the book descended into bloodstains and scribbles in the back. She imagined that must have been when the bone spurs and feathers had come. A mutation of the maalkonis, perhaps? Graudiņš had sometimes talked about mutations in plants on the farm, random changes that might make one grow bigger fruit or take on a different color. Though, whatever Dādi's old friend was going through seemed much more violent.

"That was you in the tunnels earlier today, right?" Gustavs asked. "How did you get back here?"

Karīna looked down at her hand, turning it over. The feathers and bones that protruded from it caught the torchlight. "The memory is hazy. When I tried to break through that torch's barrier, I felt its light and remembered a piece of myself. I think that I recognized you, Justīne. Your face reminded me of Oļegs'. A sliver of what I had been returned to me. When you ran, I was lost in the dark again, and I could feel the maalkonis tearing my mind apart. I stumbled and fell off the ledge. The next thing I knew, I was back here."

Gustavs raised his eyebrows at the woman but did not say anything about it.

"Have you ever seen anyone else resurrect here?" Justīne asked. "Should we be concerned about anything else leaping out of the pool?"

Karīna shrugged, the movement stiff and awkward. "I've encountered others like myself. There aren't many of us though, and most of them stick to the mountains above the tunnels. Or they roam more distant lands. But, I can't say for sure. This place operates by different rules."

Anna had pulled out the book and began reading it. Karīna reached over her shoulder, pointing at a page with a long and crooked nail. Her feathers brushed Anna's face. Justīne and Gustavs both reached for their swords, but Anna didn't even flinch.

If Karīna noticed, she didn't make it known. She said, "At this point, I was trying to use the runes to help me remember things. This one means 'recover.'" She pulled back her long hair and a few feathers on her neck, revealing an intricate scar on the side of her head. It looked old, the wound long since healed with scars black as noctis. "It did something… I remember waking up afterward and the pain searing through my bones. I don't recommend it, but I was desperate."

Anna nodded. "Were you ever successful? Even a little? Not trying to be rude, just to understand."

Pūka purred.

"It is alright." Karīna's expression became strained. "I don't remember. Glimpses, perhaps. Moments when it seemed possible to remove the maalkonis. Yes, I remember the *rush*."

She closed her eyes, exhuming some deep-rooted memory. Her hands moved in slow, asymmetrical motions. It seemed like muscle memory, violet light trailing off her fingertips. A rune hung in the air—Justīne recognized it as the rune for 'gust' that they'd seen before—and a heavy wind erupted around Karīna. It made the light of Anna's torch shudder and raised a cloud of ash that stung Justīne's skin and eyes. Through narrowed eyes, she noticed that the winds blew away the maalkonis, pushing it back beyond the perimeter of Anna's torchlight.

The dark returned in mere moments. After it did, Justīne fixed her hair, removing ash and brittle twigs from it, her eyes locked on the torch. It seemed more dim than before.

Karīna glanced down at her hands. "I was able to push it away, but only for a moment. I was never able to make the rune's effect last for more than a few heartbeats.

"When you spend enough time here, you begin to lose yourself. If the maalkonis doesn't kill you, it warps what remains. It tears your body, your memories—your very self—to ribbons. As you can see. I tried for I don't know how long to escape, to slow the changing. Eventually, I felt I'd changed too much. I couldn't focus. I couldn't remember where I'd come from or even who I was anymore. I hid my books and ran into the tunnels, hoping I'd get lost in there. Better that than risk damaging everything I'd written. Even if it never worked, the books were all I had left."

Justīne thought about how a creature—probably Karīna—had chased her and Anna through the tunnels only two years prior. She had almost caught up to them then. Justīne had the scar on her back to prove it. "You sound in control of yourself now," she said instead.

"For the most part," Gustavs added. He had sheathed his blade, but he still had a hand on the grip and stayed close enough to Karīna so that it would only take him a moment to draw steel and strike at her.

"You're right," Karīna said. "It is a struggle to remain in control, to keep my thoughts in order, but I think it's getting easier. Perhaps it is the strange torch's light or having somebody real to talk with; I don't know. My mind is clearer here. Pūka is a help, too. She has been sharing her memories of life in The Old Town. I've missed it so much. My home, the old cathedral, my neighbors."

"They're not that great," Gustavs said.

A silence passed, and Karīna's eyes became unfocused. A moment later, she sighed. "I see. The Old Town was always equal parts sanctuary and a powder keg ready to blow. I am sorry you had to endure that."

Justīne noticed the torch flicker, and the maalkonis pulsed around them as it settled. "Anna," she said, is that atstru-torch supposed to do that?"

Anna frowned and examined the device. The spinner whirred as she continued to press down the trigger. She checked a panel that rested below the guard then fiddled with the copper coil on its back. As she did, the light flickered again.

"We don't have much time," she said, her voice a little uncertain.

"What does that mean?" Gustavs asked.

"This recharges with the sun's light, and there is none out here. And the constant use…"

"How much time does it have left?" Justīne asked.

"It's hard to say. I haven't tested it under these conditions before."

"Guess."

"Maybe… I don't think we need to rush back, but we should make for The Old Town before noctis falls.

Especially considering we can't go back through the tunnels with that bridge down."

Karīna said, "There is a way around the tunnels. I can show it to you."

"That helps."

Gustavs shot Justīne a nervous glance.

"Why shouldn't we start heading back now?" Justīne asked.

"If I return to the dark," Karīna said, "I worry that it will overtake me once again." As she spoke, Pūka seemed to shiver.

"Okay," Justīne said, unsure what to do with that information. Clearly she couldn't just walk through the town's gate looking like a dead crow. Everyone would lose their minds. Justīne wasn't sure that she hadn't already.

"Well," Anna said, "If you're going to show us the way back, we should have a little time before we have to go."

"Anna," Gustaves said, his tone a warning.

"Relax," Anna said. Then to Karīna, "Can you show me the runes that you had the most success with when you were working on this? We can start with that last one you wrote. I have an idea. Do you remember Monika? She was working on this theory of pairing runes, using them to reinforce each other and focus the magic so it was less chaotic."

Karīna and Pūka's eyes narrowed in unison, sending a shiver down Justīne's spine.

"This is the basic theory," Anna said and proceeded to lecture the feathered woman in arcane theory. It was probably exactly what Monika had written in her books, and to hear Anna explain it, everything made a strange kind of sense. She spoke of the way runes exerted force, and how by having a similar force to counterbalance it, they could stabilize the effect and strengthen it all at once. She compared it to the rotary counterbalances in an atstrumeter and her atstru-torch.

When Anna finished, Justīne glanced over at Gustavs, who held a hand against the back of his head, right where she also felt a migraine coming on. But Karīna nodded slowly, stroking her chin with a bony finger.

"That's fascinating," Karīna said. "You're a mage as well then, Monika's apprentice?"

"An engineer," Anna corrected. "The maalkonis took Monika. But she wrote extensively about the arcane, and I've been reading her books."

"Amazing. Yes, I suppose… It doesn't hurt to try. Flip through those pages. I need to refresh my memory, but I have a few runes in mind that might work."

"Of course," Anna said, returning her attention to the book. "Is there anybody else out here who could help us figure this out? We need to get back as quickly as possible. Not just for our sakes but for the Ḷaodil. You know about the fighting. Dādi and Pamaman might be hurt."

"I don't think that's safe," Gustavs said.

Karīna nodded, her wet, black hair falling in front of her face. A drop of blood fell down the side of her cheek and caressed her chin in grey. She wiped it away with her thumb, careful not to claw herself.

"There are others," she said, "but it would take too long to track them down. Even then, they would see us as a threat. The maalkonis twists our minds and our perception of things, and it's hard to shake that. As you saw. My memories are coming back easier now. Give me some more time with the book. With Anna's help, maybe we can figure something out."

Karīna and Anna read through the old book together, testing different spells by drawing arcane runes in the air. When Anna asked about how that was possible, Karīna said, "Typically a mage needs something to write on, but the maalkonis has given me the ability to cast without such things. It is fortunate in a place with so little ink and parchment." She chuckled. "It is perhaps the one *gift* from this place that I actually appreciate."

They tested different pairs of runes for a while, many of which had no effect on the maalkonis. The few which did were short-lived or seemed too weak to be very useful. No matter what the runes were, Justīne noticed that, although it flickered in the presence of magic, Anna's atstru-torch burned brighter when the spells were cast.

"'Gust' and 'erase,'" Karīna said, pointing at where the runes were written in the book. "I don't remember how I figured it out, but I think that's the best one so far. I don't think they're working together particularly well, though. Let's keep 'gust' and try a few of these other runes with it."

Justīne didn't understand how they would do it, but she could see what was unfolding there in the ruined tower. If they could figure this out, it would change everything.

"Look," she said, "if you two can get this *rune pair* to work before noctis, it could be enough to stop the fighting. We can argue about who's in charge all day, but if we can show them that there's actually a way to clear away the maalkonis… Everyone wants that. Even Ievan."

Gustavs nodded. "I mean, as much as I hate to say it, this may be our only chance. But we *do* have to leave by noctis. Sooner, if that torch acts up again."

"It has been flickering a lot," Karīna said.

She looked more closely at it. Then she cast another spell, creating a small gust. The torch flickered. Karīna made another violet rune in the air, and a small fire appeared in front of her. Again, the torch flickered. Its wire burned brighter—until Karīna extinguished the magical flame she'd created.

"It's reacting to the magic," Anna said. "Why would it do that?"

Karīna shrugged. "Atstrumeters were made to react with the maalkonis, to push that back without blocking the sun or rain. Assuming this torch is built similarly, I'm not completely surprised. Even so, we should be careful."

The sky became so dark that it reminded Justīne of midnoct. Karīna assured them that it was only last dim. The words seemed hollow. The manner of which she spoke about time was The Old Town's way, but with so little light in the maalkonis, it all seemed out of place. What did first or last dim even mean in a place where the sun only created different measures of darkness?

Justīne's stomach churned. She tried to ignore it. They had nothing left to eat for vekrēla, so Gustavs offered a quick prayer without an accompanying meal, asking the Gods to see them through this safely. The rest of them, except for Karīna, echoed his words and continued about their work.

As Anna and Karīna worked, Justīne and Gustavs grew more anxious about the flickering torch. They whispered to one another, taking turns either insisting that they leave or urging patience. If Anna and Karīna could figure out those runes, it wasn't just their lives they'd save—or the whole town's. They might be able to cleanse the world of the maalkonis. Of course, that wouldn't matter if the torch failed and it killed them all. Or worse, turned them into creatures like Karīna had become, rapidly losing their minds and locked in eternal darkness. Justīne shuddered at the thought.

However, Justīne noticed how the Karīna's mutations seemed to be changing. It was hard to tell for sure, but the bone spurs appeared to be slowly receding, and she had shed multiple feathers around the ruined building. Justīne wondered if any of this was normal for her, like how Pūka shed her fur, but she didn't want to interrupt.

"What if we're thinking about this wrong?" Anna asked after several failed tests. Justīne could tell that they were frustrated by the way Anna began to pace around the room and fuss with the atstru-torch. "What if the answer's not about pushing away the maalkonis but by erasing it? Or maybe *capturing it* in something that can contain it? Like how a tree sucks up water."

Gustavs nodded. "How does this tree survive out here, anyway?" He gestured at the giant oak with violet seams.

"I don't know," Karīna said. "It was probably like me, changed by the maalkonis rather than destroyed. A glimpse of Luck's work, I suppose. Even the dark seems to give it some berth. The maalkonis is thinner around it, creating just enough space for light to come through during midday.

"The pool also has unique properties, with the ability to rejuvenate and heal things affected by the maalkonis. I don't remember when I found it, but I do remember drinking from it, and afterward, I've felt linked to it in a way that I can't describe. It is a magic much older than these runes. I think it's also why my magic is this strong here. I was not a very skilled mage while I was living in The Old Town."

Karīna frowned, her brow furrowed as she gazed at the massive oak. Anna seemed to take notice and stood up to join her, holding the torch up to its cracking bark. Pūka leapt onto one of the boughs beside her, walking up it.

"If the tree repels the maalkonis, and the water it drinks has healing properties, I wonder if we could use it somehow," Anna said. Her torch seemed to brighten beside it.

"The torch is having some kind of reaction to it," Justīne said.

Anna drew the torch away from the massive tree, and the light dimmed, almost imperceptibly. When she moved it closer, it seemed to burn more brightly.

Karīna said, "What if… What if the atstru-torch and the magic in the tree are like a rune pair. Two things with similar effects on the maalkonis, stronger when combined."

"How would you combine your torch and a tree like that?" Gustavs said, the hint of a laugh on his words.

Anna said, "I could carve a piece of the wood for a new handle, but I don't have the tools for that here."

"It's bleeding sap from those cracks in the bark," Justīne said.

Anna leaned in closer to one of the violet fissures in the tree. "If we could collect that, I might be able to use it as a kind of ink. Karīna, do you think that writing these runes in the sap of a tree imbued with ancient magic might empower them?"

Karīna looked at her quizzically. Through Pūka, she said, "There is a power to the way magic is expressed. My mother called it a 'force of will.' It could be expressed through the mage's intent but also their instruments—ink included. But the writing itself doesn't necessarily have to be in ink. That's where we got blood magic, people who believed that writing in blood would create more powerful spells. Perhaps using the sap would do something. But I do not understand the tree's magic, nor your torch, well enough to say what. But perhaps blood magic was never any more or less powerful than regular ink runes."

"There's never been a tree like this before, though," Anna said. To Justīne, she said, "Can I borrow your sword?"

"It was damaged in the maalkonis," she said, revealing the jagged tip.

Anna turned the blade over, regarding it with a frown. "Huh. It's like a needle."

"Looks easier to pierce the bark with." Gustavs shrugged.

Anna took the blade and drove it into the oak, pushing the steel between its massive plates of bark into one of the violet fissures between them. Sap oozed slowly onto the flat of the blade. Then, around it, green stems emerged from the sword, blossoming into rows of tiny red, violet, and white flowers.

Pūka sat up, and Karīna's voice spoke through her, "I don't think I've seen it do that before."

Noctis crept across the sky like a whisper. Justīne didn't notice when, only that at some point no light remained in the sky. It had already been dark, but it was as if the skies themselves conspired to render her blind. There was no familiar haze that normally came in The Old Town. In comparison, Anna's torch seemed blinding, its light unbearably bright against the sheer darkness that enveloped them. Yet, they knew it had become weaker since they set out into the dark at first dim. The sanctuary it provided was noticeably smaller than before, forcing them to crowd in closer toward it. They would have to leave soon or risk the light failing altogether.

Anna tore a strip of bark from the ancient oak and cleaned off the inside as best she could. She deposited the sap she collected there, wiping the flat of Niklāvs' sword on it. She began testing different rune pairs with it, using one of Karīna's feathers to write on the torch directly, the shaft cut to a point with Gustavs' sword. While she tried different runes, Justīne made sure Anna had plenty of sap, collecting a small basin of it in the sheet of bark. It was clear and sticky, with dirt and splinters suspended inside of it. It gave off an odd, violet sheen when the light struck it just right.

Anna used her pen to drag the massive oak's sap across the copper head of the torch, its gears still spinning and the copper wire still burning. She complained about how difficult it was to place the sap where she wanted, but Karīna didn't seem particularly concerned. She instructed Anna to make corrections as needed, looking over Anna's shoulder intently.

Justīne could not deny the sense of hope that filled her as she watched her little sister and the feathered creature work together. Even if the spell didn't *keep* the maalkonis away, this felt like the closest anyone had ever come to beating it back. Not only delaying the inevitable but actually fighting against it. Thank the Gods that Anna was so stubborn, continuing to read Monika's books and pushing them to explore the maalkonis. They never would have made it this far without her. Not even close.

If this did work, Justīne could scarcely imagine what would happen next. Their parents and neighbors had stories of the world as it was before, but those stories had always felt like a dream to her, akin to tales of mischievous faeries and shape-shifting laumas disguised as histories. She wondered if, like Anna's torch at this hour, the sun would be *too* bright without the maalkonis between it and the world. Would her crops burn without the shade of the maalkonis? She knew that she should be excited, but the uncertainty of a world without the dark also frightened her.

Anna finished drawing the runes for 'gust' and 'disperse.' They created a sudden burst of wind, tearing at everything around the torch. Justīne felt the cool air and ash tearing at her face. It had an effect on the maalkonis as well, but it was temporary and caused more damage to their surroundings due to the high winds, threatening to extinguish the wire burning at the top of the torch. Anna wiped off the runes and worked with Karīna to find a new pair to test.

The 'break' and 'sun' runes made the torch glow a blinding, white light, expanding the torch's sanctuary, holding back more of the maalkonis. But the gears in the machine began to strain. When the light faded, the sanctuary returned to its regular size, and the darkness rolled back in just as quickly.

'Fire' and 'sunder' cast sparks all around them, singing their clothes and skin. Another attempt that Anna had to quickly dismantle, wiping the sap off so that she could try again. Clearly the magic was having an effect, but none were what they needed.

"Try this," Karīna said, pointing at some runes in the old book. "'Beckon' and 'erase.' The pair isn't as similar as some of the others, but like you said before, maybe we're thinking about this the wrong way. Instead of punching at the maalkonis, try to draw it in to remove it."

"Right," Anna said and began copying the runes onto the torch.

"Whether this one works or not"—Gustavs paused to yawn—"we should pack up and start moving toward The Old Town after. It's getting late, and the torch's light has looked better."

Anna didn't respond. Justīne wiped the sap off Niklāvs' sword as best she could and sheathed it. The little well Anna had made wouldn't hold any more sap, and Gustavs was right. With every attempt, the atstru-torch was flickering more and getting dimmer despite Anna's quick reaction to remove the runes when they clearly failed. They didn't have much time left.

"In fact"—Gustavs glanced up at the black sky—"we should probably have left already."

"Give them one more try," Justīne said.

"I'm almost done," Anna said, drawing the final marks on her torch. There was a moment of silence as she adjusted the sap. Then the torch's copper gears began to spin faster and the light burned more brightly. Justīne had to avert her eyes. When she did, she saw how the maalkonis shuddered around them. Karīna wailed as inky ribbons of darkness were ripped from her body and pulled into the torch. Shreds of the maalkonis came from all around them. Above, the sun's light grew a little brighter. Justīne caught a glimpse of it, a white orb in the black sky.

Anna's arm shook as the gears in the torch screamed, a piercing, tumultuous sound that mingled with a distant roar. Or perhaps the torch's song was echoing off the walls and hills, shaking the ground beneath their feet. Even as it did, green shoots sprouted from between the rotting wood, brick, and stone. Pūka ran to Justīne and leapt into her arms. The cat's claws dug into her shoulder, and her tail was low and bristly. The darkness was being pulled from her body as well. She shook like Justīne had never seen the brave cat do before, and Karīna's cries thundered through her.

Anna swiped the torch with her hand, smearing the sap. The maalkonis rolled in around them, enveloping the sanctuary that the torch's light cast and dimming the sun once again. When she moved a step to the side, the gap in the maalkonis remained where the torch had been activated with the runes. Like a hole punched out of the world, Anna looked over at Justīne, a peculiar expression on her face. Justīne noticed that the changes Pūka had endured due to her brief time in the maalkonis were gone. Her ashy coat was mostly replaced by her usual rusty orange color.

Karīna also appeared slightly more human. The bone spurs had receded further, and her skin looked less pale. She still bore her claws and violet eyes, as well as a few feathers on her arms, but it seemed as though the runic torch had helped pull her back from whatever monstrosity the maalkonis had turned her into.

"I need to know..." Anna said, staring at Justīne.

It was too late before Justīne realized what her sister intended. She broke into a run to stop Anna, but Anna turned off the torch before Justīne could reach her.

The light vanished. Justīne held tightly onto Pūka and braced herself for the maalkonis' grasp—but it never came. Even after what must have been several long minutes under a haze of near-light that came from above the maalkonis. Pūka mewed and leapt from her arms. Justīne felt her claws catch her arm, but that was it. It was dark, almost impossible to see anything, but the deathly touch of the maalkonis never came.

"It works," Anna said, and the torch came back on. A bright smile crossed Anna's lips. Dark circles hung under her eyes, and she stood lethargically, but practically shook with excitement.

"You could have gotten us all killed," Justīne shouted at her. "What were you thinking?"

"Karīna said historically the effect was short-lived. I needed to know if that was still the case, or if the torch and sap helped *keep* it at bay."

Justīne huffed at her. She wanted to yell and throw a fit. Anna had endangered them all—and herself—and Justīne wanted to rip her head off for that…

…But Anna had also done the impossible. It had actually worked. They had a way to force back the maalkonis. For good.

"Why did you remove the rune?" Gustavs asked. By his tone, Justīne thought it sounded like he was wrestling with the same frustration as her.

Justīne looked at the barrier that the torch emitted and noticed that she was closer to the edge than she'd been before. She took a step closer to the center and said, "The torch is getting dimmer."

Anna collected herself and nodded. "It should have enough power to make that trip and still put on a quick show for everyone there. I'll reapply the runes when we arrive. Until then, I don't want to stress it. Thank you for teaching me how to draw the runes, Karīna."

"That was perfect," Karīna said through Pūka.

The cat purred from a perch it had found atop a fallen rafter.

"I think I could almost see the sun," Justīne said. "I didn't realize it stayed out through noctis."

"That wasn't the sun," Karīna said. "Normally you can't see it through the maalkonis, even in The Old Town, but my mother used to tell me about another celestial force, one which used to mean a great deal to people before the darkness spread. She called it 'mūnes,' or the moon."

IV

The four of them, with Pūka at their heels, set off for The Old Town. They moved at a brisk walk. Nobody wanted to spend the night out in the maalkonis, and Anna's torch was flickering even more. It had gotten weaker since they'd left the ancient oak tree, its sanctuary now only a few meters wide. They walked shoulder-to-shoulder, careful not to get too close to the edge where—when the light flickered—the maalkonis surged toward them. It never got far, but they knew better than to risk it. Karīna had become the most sheepish among them, audibly gasping sometimes when the light faltered.

Justīne felt her limbs dragging, the weight of Niklāvs' sword heavy on her hip. They'd been on the run for a full day with hardly a moment of rest, unless one counted standing guard for monsters in the dark as *rest*. Still, if this worked, it would all have been worth it. The maalkonis was no longer just a place to hide. It had provided the very antidote they'd been praying for from the Gods, prayers that spanned generations. Funny, Justīne thought, how what they'd needed to disperse the inky darkness was something they could only find in its choking grasp.

As they walked, Anna kept Karīna's book of research and runes close to her chest. She read from it as they walked, motioning with her feather pen in the air. Karīna insisted that Anna learn the 'beckon' and 'erase' runes that had proved so effective. The woman's hands—her claws—made it difficult to hold the pen, and she worried that Anna might need to draw them quickly when they reached the town. Occasionally, Anna asked Karīna a question about writing runes, and the woman confirmed or corrected her.

Gustavs watched the horizon, as much as was possible in the dark, his hand on his sword at all times. He seemed as tired as Justīne felt, but he remained on guard. She glanced at the wound on his arm, which Karīna had given him and which Justīne had bound in the scraps of her tunic. His blood had stained the wrappings, leaking red.

The rotten bridge in the tunnels was too heavily damaged to cross again. Gustavs suggested walking right up to the town's main gate, across the corroded copper bridge. The way to the bridge was longer than the path through the tunnels. Karīna led them around several large hills, through a narrow pass, and only then could they begin walking toward the town. She insisted this was better than the more direct route over the hills.

"We can handle a little climb," Gustavs said of the detour.

"It is not the mountains I worry about, kittens. Rather, the creatures that prowl there at noctis. I could not fight them off should they break through the torch's light."

"Did you call us *kittens*?" Gustavs glared between the cat and Karīna.

Pūka purred, and Karīna said, "Trust me. You have already come so far. Do not risk throwing all this away simply to arrive a bit sooner."

Justīne asked, "I thought you said earlier that nobody else was out here?"

"No, I said nobody could help us."

Anna nodded. "When we're finished, we'll have to help them too."

Karīna regarded her with a dull violet eye. "I hope that you can, Anna. But make sure you are armor-clad. Not everyone out here is as considerate as I am. They don't all have fond memories of The Old Town to call upon. If they have any memories left at all."

Anna shrugged. "Killing you seemed to make you quite considerate. Downright pleasant, I'd say."

Pūka purred, glancing back at Anna for a moment. Justīne wondered if that was the cat's doing or Karīna's. When this was over, and she'd finally gotten some sleep, she would have to ask exactly how that spell of hers worked. And if their connection went both ways, perhaps Karīna could explain to the little beast exactly how important it was that she catch all the mice around the farm.

But first, she supposed they should focus on saving the world.

Her siblings were hesitant to put a voice to the hope that she knew they felt. Karīna had simply urged them on. Given the way her body had mutated out in the maalkonis for so long, Justīne still couldn't tell what she was thinking. It was easier for her to read how the damned cat was feeling.

Justīne couldn't fathom how Karīna had persisted after all that she'd been through, but a bit more color had returned to her skin, and the violet veins which ran up her arms only stretched as far as her wrists and ankles. The patch on her neck had receded so much that it was completely hidden by her long hair. With each passing hour, she seemed more human. The light of Anna's torch was doing *something* to her body and mind, not just giving her clarity over her own memories. It also appeared to be healing her.

⌒

Once they made it around the tunnels and the mountains above them, Karīna led the way through a field filled with the husks of trees burnt and broken by the maalkonis. She called it a *mortežs*—a dead forest. It lived up to the name; there must have been thousands of trees, more than Justīne had ever seen, and none had survived. They still stood tall but were barren of leaves and looked as though they were made of shattered glass, given the way jagged pieces had been broken off and had scattered to the wind.

Justīne accidentally brushed up against one of their branches, and it disintegrated into ash, marking the sleeve of her tunic with a black stain. She found herself dreaming of a proper bath and change of clothes.

The Old Town appeared on the horizon. It was a blurry, almost imperceptible smudge of light in a world of darkness and obscured by the crooked boughs of dead trees. As they approached, Justīne heard the river. It bubbled and gurgled over stones and around the bridge that she knew was there but could not yet see. Justīne wanted to run on ahead, but she reminded herself that she needed to stay within the dimming light of Anna's torch.

Even if she could run, Justīne worried that her knees would buckle, and she'd embarrass herself. Her stomach was past growling and simply hurt. Moving made it worse. Breathing made it worse. She considered asking the others to stop and rest, but she wasn't sure how much longer Anna's torch would last. And if she did lay down, Justīne wasn't sure she'd have the strength to get back up. So, she kept her eyes fixed on the dim glow of the town's copper torches and put one foot in front of the other. She hummed an old song, something she knew in her bones but couldn't put words to. It had a rhythm that she liked.

"Stop," Gustavs spat after a few seconds. "I don't want to hear a *funeral song* right now."

"Sorry," Justīne said, rubbing her eyes. "I didn't even realize that was what it was."

"It's a wedding song too," Anna reminded them.

"It doesn't matter," Justīne said. "It's just a stupid song. I wasn't thinking about it. Let's just keep moving."

❧

They found the river and followed it downstream. Justīne fidgeted with the pommel of Niklāvs' sword as she dragged her feet forward. At some point, air became slightly less oppressive. Rather than a pitch-black curtain above them, the maalkonis took on a heavy grey color, with a rosy haze on the horizon. Justīne could see the violet wisps swirling around the maalkonis again. The sun must have risen. The Old Town would soon be awake, beginning their work for the day. Assuming that the fighting was over.

Justīne had to imagine that, after all this time, somebody had come out victorious. The town wasn't very large, and there were few places to shelter or hide. She and Anna were the only ones who'd known how to escape. Either Ievan and those who sided with him had seized control, or they'd been beaten. Justīne prayed for the latter, but either way, she was confident that once they saw Anna clear away the maalkonis, they'd think twice about shooting anyone.

Justīne spared a thought for poor Niklāvs, who'd been shot dead on the farmhouse's doorstep. After he'd so kindly volunteered to stand watch that night.

She also worried about Dādi and especially Ešlija, who'd fought so hard to keep her safe. She thought Dādi might be okay—even if Ievan came out victorious, he'd know that they would need Dādi to maintain the atstrumeters. However, Ešlija would be a threat to him: a skilled fighter who had opposed him and Lilija at every step.

Even Kriŝs, Teodor, and everyone else who supported the rebellion earned a degree of Justīne's sympathies. She could understand their fears and anxieties, even if they were misplaced. She'd wanted to cut them all down a day ago, but there were so few Ļaodil left, and there was so little that the maalkonis hadn't taken from them. That was why she'd tried so hard to get ahead of the problem when she noticed the shortages in the farmhouse cellar. They could have gotten through the winter together if everyone had tried to make it work. She had to hope that they could get past this and rebuild the trust they used to have. Otherwise, what was the point of all this?

However, it occurred to her that if they hadn't rebelled, Anna never would have asked them to flee through the tunnels with her in the first place. At least, in any other circumstance, Justīne was sure she'd do everything in her power to stop her sister. They likely never would have found Karīna or discovered the way that runes—written in the sap of that ancient oak—could empower Anna's atstru-torch. Ievan and Lilija's dissent might be the very thing that saved The Old Town.

Justīne refused to be thankful for the way they spread lies and bloodshed, and she could not forgive them. She could not help but wonder if this were some cruel and poetic game fashioned by the Gods, of which she'd been made a pawn. She hoped that, since the thought was not given in prayer or over a meal, they would not notice she'd had it.

Justīne heard the din of several atstrumeters before she noticed the bridge of copper and stone. She could make out a hazy light above moving left to right. She guessed that their torch had been spotted by a guard, and they were following along the wall. Good. It would save them the time of trying to catch the town's attention.

They arrived at the stone and copper bridge which crossed the river. Gustavs noticed the corpse beside first. It lay beside the bridge, as if the person had collapsed after crossing it. It was a tall young man. His hair was singed, and his skin was pale. Blood drenched one side of his tunic, and he had fallen among the bones of others who had been exiled or let the maalkonis take their lives at that same spot.

Gustavs took the corpse by the chin and lifted the man's head. "Ievan," he said.

The smith's eyes were open, unblinking. One of his irises had changed to a bright violet. Whatever had happened, the maalkonis had been changing him before he died. Perhaps he just couldn't take the transformation, or it had burned him alive before he could see it through. For every tree like the violet-lined oak, there were thousands dead like those in the mortežs.

"They must have cast him out," Justīne said.

"I never thought it would come to this. Even when he took up that Gods-damned rifle, I thought *maybe* he could be talked down. He wasn't always a bastard."

Justīne considered arguing, because she absolutely felt as though his death was deserved. For what he did, she would have liked to throw him into the maalkonis herself. But she decided to keep that to herself. Gustavs was still clinging to memories of growing up with Ievan.

Gustavs asked, "June, will you help me move him out of the way?"

They moved Ievan's body to the side of the bridge, laying him on the ash and dirt.

Karīna asked, "Do you need a moment to make a cairn for your friend?"

Justīne barked a mirthless laugh. "If it were up to me, we'd clear this place of the maalkonis and leave him so that the crows may peck out his eyes more easily."

Karīna's eyes widened at her.

Gustavs grimaced at her. "Hells, June. He should have a proper pyre. Despite everything, everyone deserves a chance to see the Bright Garden."

Justīne glared at him.

Gustavs continued, "But now isn't the time for any of that. Let's go home first and figure out what's happened. Maybe take a nap."

Justīne nodded, glancing around the dead land and rusty bridge. A nap sounded incredible; her bones ached for it, but she could not help but think of all that they still needed to do. Trials for the rebels, a study of the atstru-torch and the runes. Not to mention all of their normal, day-to-day work. "There will be a lot to clean up around here."

Pūka nuzzled her ankle. She picked the cat up and walked toward the bridge, stopping at the end of the torch's light. Anna joined her there and the rest followed.

"At least we know there are friends across that bridge," Anna said, her voice taught with nerves. "Are you ready?"

"I should be asking you that," Justīne said, scratching the cat's chin. "You're the one who's doing all the hard work."

Gustavs asked Anna, "Do you need a moment to practice or prepare anything?"

Anna held up the quill pen they'd made by the oak. Its tip was already primed with sap from the batch they'd collected, clear and shining in the torch's light.

"All ready," she said. "It won't take long, either. I just need to redraw the runes."

"If anything goes wrong," Karīna said, "I should be able to help hold the maalkonis at bay. I can't hold a barrier or completely disperse it the way you can, but I can buy you a few seconds at least." She drew her hands into an arc. Violet light trailed from her claws. "Not much, I know."

"I appreciate it." Anna breathed.

Justīne could hear more people talking along the wall. She couldn't tell who was there, but their voices carried through the maalkonis.

"Looks like we're already gathering an audience," Justīne said. "They can probably see your torchlight."

"We're not exactly being quiet, either," Anna said. "Should we wait until more gather and see this? I don't know if I will be able to repeat this. The torch is almost out of power; it needs to sit in the light and recharge."

"Best just get it over with," Gustavs said. "One of them might get nervous and shoot at us."

Karīna nodded. "Honestly, shooting things that move around in the maalkonis is wise life advice. If you've got the powder to spare."

Anna took a few deep breaths, her eyes on the horizon, on the space above the bridge. The maalkonis filled the air, but after only a few paces forward, they'd step out into the narrow space around The Old Town.

"We've got your back," Justīne said.

Pūka leapt out of her arms and looked up at Anna, her tail twitching.

"Thank you," Anna said. She knelt down to pet the cat. Then when Anna was ready, they stepped forward together.

Though the light emitted by her torch had diminished, the maalkonis parted around them. The darkness in front of them grew thin as they crossed the bridge. Justīne could see through it, toward The Old Town, though she could only spot the brick wall and the old gate set into it. Four people stood on the walkway, but she could hear others moving and shouting behind the wall. As Justīne's eyes adjusted to the light, she recognized their faces. The two who had drawn their swords were Aleks and Bruno, who surely had volunteered to help the fractured guard keep watch. She had no doubts that several were chained up somewhere or killed in the fighting. A third guard—Ešlija—leveled an arquebus at them as they crossed the bridge. Justīne was about to call out to her when she noticed the man holding a torch at her side.

"Dādi," Justīne said, relief flooding her bones.

Dādi was safe. Her pamaman was safe. They both looked exhausted and terrified, but they were *alive*. The Old Town and the Ļaodil were surely a mess inside those walls, but all things considered, Justīne was awash with relief.

The panic that rose in Dādi and Ešlija's voices was immediate and inconsolable. Dādi waved his torch, and they shouted together, "Run!"

Before Justīne could say anything, a crack thundered through the air, and black smoke erupted around Ešlija, obscuring her face in darkness. In the same moment, Justīne heard Karīna gasp behind her. She spun to see the woman collapse, grasping at her chest.

Dādi yelled, "To the gate!" and sprinted toward the nearest stairs.

"Hells, Mama!" Gustavs shouted.

"Don't shoot!" Anna yelled at the wall. Then, to Karīna, she asked, "Can you stand? You're almost there."

"June," Gustavs said, "we need to get her to Sofija."

He grabbed Karīna's legs, and Justīne took her by the arms. Together, they lifted and carried her across the rest of the bridge, stopping only once they were fully out of the maalkonis. Black and red blood seeped between Karīna's fingers, swirling together. It dripped over the bridge and grass.

"Get away from that thing," Ešlija shouted and began reloading. To Dādi and the guards she commanded, "Do not let that *creature* get inside."

"Stop!" Anna shouted back at them. "Karīna is helping us!"

The guards on the other side of the wall paused, glancing at them then one another. Justīne couldn't see Dādi's face, but she swore that she heard him utter Karīna's name.

Karīna said, "This isn't what I had in mind when I suggested shooting at things in the maalkonis." Pūka's voice sounded hoarse and distant. "I don't know what the pool's limits are, you know. Not something I've thought to test."

"You're going to be fine," Justīne said, ignoring the tears in her eyes. "Sofija's an excellent surgeon. She'll get the ball out and stitch you up so fast. We just need to get you to her."

She and Gustavs tried to carry her toward the gate, but Karīna gripped a rung of the bridge's rail, preventing them from pulling her any further.

"Poultices and herbs won't stem a wound like this. Not quickly… Enough," she said. Her breathing was becoming more labored already. "The maalkonis. It will repair my body."

"The same maalkonis that you said tore apart your mind, right?" Gustavs asked.

Karīna smiled sadly. "It's risky, but it's the only way. I'm losing… Losing too much blood." She raised a hand off her wound, and blood surged forth around her fingers. She rubbed them together, staring at the swirls of black and red. Her long fingernails—no longer claws—clicked together as she did. "I may not be myself after. I am so sorry, but if I cannot regain control after it heals me, do not hesitate to kill me. An arquebus' ball. Or blade to the heart. That should do it. Do not let me hurt anyone."

They set Karīna down. Justīne didn't know what to say. She glanced at Gustavs for help, but he looked as though he was in shock. Justīne glanced back at the wall, to where Ešlija and Dādi both stood again. They looked as though they were in shock as well.

"Don't do this. Don't let her do this," Anna pleaded with Karīna then tugged on Justīne's arm. "I will follow you into the dark if you try."

"Sweet Anna," Karīna said. A tear formed in her violet eyes as she caressed Anna's cheek. "Thank you for never giving up. For finding my book. Hold onto it tight."

Swifter than Justīne thought possible, Karīna made a rune with her hands. Violet light dashed the air before them. Propelled by some unseen force, she leapt out of the torch's sanctuary and back across the bridge, so fast that she became a blur of light. Justīne heard a collective gasp from the people on the wall. Anna tried to run after her, but Justīne grabbed her by the arm and held her back.

"She's already gone," Justīne said. "Give her a moment to heal."

"Prepare the runes," Gustavs told Anna, and he drew his sword. "Once you're ready, we'll go in after her. If we have any chance at rescuing her, we'll need the torch to purge the dark from her body again."

Anna shook off Justīne's grip, but she stayed put. "I don't like it."

"You have a better idea?"

Anna said nothing. She only withdrew the sap that she'd collected from the oak and her quill pen.

Justīne drew Niklāvs' sword and called back to Ešlija. She gestured at the maalkonis with the blade's shattered tip. "That creature was Ļaodil once. One of our neighbors. Her name is Karīna, and she needs our help. The maalkonis will bar her from approaching, but Anna's torch can open up a path. If we cannot calm her, we will force her back into the dark. If that fails, we need to be ready to fight."

"We don't know exactly what she can do," Gustavs spoke up, his voice hoarse. "Have your swords and arquebuses at the ready, but do not shoot unless one of us tells you to. Do not charge, as you may be lost to the dark or accidentally let her in. Somebody prepare to open the gate. Be ready if we need a quick escape, but keep it locked for now. Do you understand?"

"Gav," Ešlija said, "what—"

"Listen to them!" Anna shouted.

Justīne glanced at her sister, whose hands were sticky with sap and her dress marred by ash. Tears glistened in Anna's furious eyes. She pressed her feather pen to the torch, bending the tip as she drew the runes. What a mess the three of them must look. They'd run through the tunnels, stayed awake all night, and now they returned covered in ash with clothes torn, and then they returned alongside a creature from the maalkonis. And all after The Old Town had put itself to the sword and flame.

She should have expected this. They should have planned for it. Justīne had been so focused on the amazing feat that Karīna and Anna had accomplished. She was so exhausted and so used to being around Karīna, that they forgot how godsdamn terrible first impressions of the woman were. She was the very thing they'd all learned to fear. Despite the fact she'd slowly begun to look less monstrous, to the rest of the Ļaodil, she was still their mythical creature from the maalkonis. She was their fears made real.

Dādi put a hand on Ešlija's shoulder and said, "Anna's been studying Monika's books for years. If anyone can do this, I trust her."

Anna's eyes went wide, and she paused her drawing. She glanced back at him and asked, "You knew?"

"Of course I knew." He smiled, then his expression fell into one of worry. "Why do you think I kept reminding you how dangerous it was? Just tell me, is there another way?"

Anna shook her head.

"Alright." He turned to Ešlija. "Then we need to let them work."

Ešlija shared a glance with Dādi. They spoke a few words, too quiet and too distant for Justīne to hear. Then Ešlija finished loading her arquebus, a steely resolve falling over her face.

"Guards!" she shouted. "If you have an arquebus, get on the wall and prepare to fire. Hold for Justīne or Gustavs' command. If you do not have an arquebus, prepare your blade and get down by the gate. You will not charge out front unless you are needed. When called upon, open the door but do not let that *thing* inside. Everyone else, go to your homes and bar the doors shut."

"Are you sure?" Aleks said, his voice catching.

"I trust them."

They whispered back and forth for a moment longer, then silence settled in, and the wall was a flurry of activity. The arquebusiers formed a line, a few of them loading their guns. Guards without one hurried to the gate, and everyone else who had come to see the commotion disappeared behind the wall.

Ešlija gave Justīne, Anna, and Gustavs a curt nod.

"Thank you," Justīne called up to her.

"We'll need answers later," she said sternly.

"You'll have them," Gustavs said. "I promise."

"Oh," Anna said, "would somebody let the cat back in?" There was a moment of silence, then the gate opened just enough for Pūka to run through. Then it closed again. They heard the latch shut with a wooden *thud*. Anna called after them, "And will somebody feed her?"

Justīne exhaled. She hadn't realized she'd been holding her breath. She and Gustavs took up defensive stances, their blades pointed toward the maalkonis. Justīne heard running behind the wall and on the walkway and Dādi's voice as he spoke with somebody. She dared not pull her gaze away from the cloud of whirling inky darkness. Karīna would no doubt be changed by her reemergence into it. They would have to pull her back as they had accidentally done by the ancient oak tree. They knew what they were doing this time, sort of, but would they be able to save her the same way as before? The maalkonis seemed so temperamental. Would it affect Karīna in the same ways or do something new?

They also didn't have access to the pool beside the oak, or any more of its sap. Perhaps Anna's torch and the runes she drew on it would help, as it seemed to reduce the mutations on Karīna before, but how far would that go? And how much of Karīna's sanity would remain? Would she recognize them as friends or see their swords and Dādi aiming at her from upon the wall and lash out? Would she even be able to leave the maalkonis this time?

Anna wrote on her torch with the oak's sap, the feather pen scraping against copper. The seconds dragged on like days, and sweat formed along Justīne's brow. The pain in her stomach reminded her how little she'd eaten, and the stinging in her eyes reminded her that she'd been awake since first dim the prior day.

Then, a movement in the dark. The maalkonis itself seemed to roil around whatever moved inside.

"There she is," Gustavs said, adjusting his grip on his sword.

Justīne tried to quiet her mind and focus on the task at hand. They would return to the maalkonis one more time. Whatever happened next, they would deal with it together. Then she would have a nice long bath.

"I'll never forgive Dādi if she doesn't make it," Anna said, her voice quivering. "I'm almost done. 'Erase' takes a while to write. I'm sorry."

A violet glare appeared through the maalkonis. Karīna must have been no more than a meter or two from the edge. Justīne took a deep breath. The river made a gentle sound as it parted around the bridge.

An animalistic, chittering growl filled the air, and her violet gaze raised up, higher than should have been possible. Then it disappeared.

Justīne said, "Anna, I think we're losing her."

"In more ways than one," Gustavs added.

"Hold on," Anna said, bent over the torch.

Then she raised it triumphantly and flicked a switch all in one motion. The gears inside the copper head of the torch whirred back to life. Its light shot out like daggers, and rather than repel the maalkonis, the light seemed to pull it in. Black ribbons tore away from the dark clouds and were reeled into the light of her torch, which seemed to burn even brighter. Behind them, a chorus of shock and awe arose from the guards. Good, Justīne thought. They would still see Anna's work firsthand.

Anna walked forward, and a cavity formed in the darkness over the bridge. The gears inside of the torch spun faster, and the light flickered, but she pressed on. Gasps and shouting erupted from behind them, even louder as the maalkonis was ripped apart wherever the torch's light reached. Justīne caught Dādi's voice among them, but not what he said.

She ignored them and moved in step with her sister, Gustavs taking up a spot on Anna's other side. Ribbons of darkness sped past Justīne, cutting and stinging her skin. It was nothing compared to the hunger that gnawed at her stomach or the exhaustion in her bones. They pressed on together.

They reached the other end of the bridge, and Justīne caught sight of two violet eyes. She pointed them out to Anna, and she ran in their direction. Their sprint took Karīna by surprise, it seemed, as the light knocked her backward.

Justīne hesitated as she beheld the creature in front of them. Its black feathers, protruding bones, and violet veins were reminiscent of Karīna's, but the maalkonis had turned her into something completely different—and much larger. Her neck was elongated, her face more reminiscent of a snake's than a human's. She had a mouth now, but her jaw was bloody and fangs jutted in awkward angles. She had a long tail, the end of it thin as wire, and her skin seemed to be made up of charcoal-grey scales. From her back, two wings had sprouted, similar to those of a crow's, with long feathers black as noctis. Karīna stood on hands and legs, which now resembled a large cat's paws, with long jagged claws. She bared her teeth, revealing long white fangs and a serpent's tongue. A light appeared in her throat, and bright orange flames rushed toward them.

Justīne leapt to the side. When she looked over her shoulder, she saw Gustavs with his back turned, black scorch marks across his tunic and rosy burns on his shoulder. The bandage she'd wrapped around his arm was aflame, and he quickly tore it off.

Anna was on the ground beside him. She still held the atstru-torch, which flickered maddeningly.

"Hells," Justīne cursed and ran to help her up. As she did, she told her sister, "We need to get out of here."

"No," Anna said.

Anna directed the torch at Karīna, and ribbons of darkness ripped away from her body. Karīna reared and slashed at Anna with long claws. Justīne put herself between them, raising Niklāvs' broken sword. The impact shattered the tip of the blade, exposing a bright violet core within the steel.

When Karīna swiped at them again, Gustavs blocked it with his sword. The two were locked in a contest of strength, neither budging. Justīne heard an arquebus crack—followed by the thunderous pop of at least two others. They hadn't listened to her, apparently, but if they hit their mark, they didn't seem to faze the creature Karīna had become, though Justīne could see that the arquebus wound from Ešlija's first shot was still bleeding. The scales around it hadn't fully formed, and black blood dripped down her chest and arm.

Karīna snarled at them, an orange light emerging from her fanged maw, as Justīne rushed forward. She leapt and stabbed Niklāvs' sword—though it had been reduced to the length of a dagger—into her wound. The fire in Karīna's maw came out as spittle, stinging Justīne's arm when the creature roared.

Gustavs took advantage of the way Karīna stumbled and moved forward, slashing up and down one of her arms. He struck at Karīna's joints, landing a series of rapid cuts. Justīne wrenched the blade from Karīna's chest and followed Gustavs' lead, striking at the monstrous thing's wings and legs from the other side. Her blade was black with blood. Karīna stumbled, breathing heavily.

"Anna," Justīne shouted, "if you're going to do something, it needs to happen *now*."

"I don't know what else to do!" Anna shouted back. She advanced on Karīna anyway, using the torch to pull the maalkonis out of her. She was teary-eyed and fiercely determined. Justīne could see the color return to Karīna's skin, her lizard-like scales shimmering, and feathers fell from her wings. A few of them burnt up in the maalkonis as they left the torch's light. Karīna wailed and lashed out at them. Justīne and Gustavs blocked her attacks, but only just. The sheer force of them left Justīne winded. She needed a shield, not a broken sword.

Fire sputtered out of Karīna's mouth. Justīne had time to shove Anna out of the way, but the flames licked Justīne's arm. Part of it felt numb; other parts stung. Her eyes watered at the heat and pain, but she stood her guard and deflected another swipe of Karīna's paw when Justīne tried to gore her.

Gustavs yelled. Justīne looked just in time to see that Karīna's tail had whipped him. Gustavs collapsed, and a swift swipe from Karīna's paw sent Anna to the ground. Karīna roared triumphantly.

"Anna!" Justīne shouted as the atstru-torch's light flickered, its radius no longer any more than an arm's length. The maalkonis around them crept closer, even as the torch removed it. "It's over. I'm sorry. Get Gustavs out of here."

Anna held the torch up to Karīna, stumbling to her feet. She had a litany of bloody scratches. Gustavs wasn't moving. Anna glanced between her and Gustavs' crumpled form. The torch still pulled the maalkonis and whatever darkness infested Karīna, but whatever it was doing wasn't fast or strong enough. Justīne could see the same recognition in Anna's eyes as the determination behind them diminished. Then, as the torchlight flickered, it finally gave out. The torch was drained, and the maalkonis—fractured as it was—surrounded them. The silence of it was deafening.

"I can't leave you alone," Anna said, breathing heavily.

"I'll be right behind you. I promise."

She didn't respond, but Justīne heard Anna drag Gustavs' body past Ievan's corpse and across the bridge. The maalkonis settled, falling closer with the atstru-torch gone, but it only advanced a short distance. Plenty of room for Justīne to hold Karīna off safely.

Justīne rushed toward Karīna, slashing at her arms and chest, pushing her back. All she had to do was force her back into the maalkonis. Maybe if she could do that, Karīna would be trapped in the dark. If she could do that, they could still rescue her later once they'd recharged the torch.

Another chorus of arquebuses fired. This time, Justīne counted at least five thunderous pops. She could smell the black powder in the air, and she saw at least one hit their mark. This time, black blood dripped from a fresh wound in Karīna's shoulder. Her feathers dripped in it. Karīna roared and—before Justīne realized it—picked her up. Karīna's wings flared, and she leapt, ascending into the sky.

Justīne felt the rush of air around her and nothing beneath her feet. Karīna's claws pierced through her tunic. The light of first dim flickered out all around her as they soared into the maalkonis. Dark clouds choked her, burning like she stood at the center of a pyre. It felt as though there was a fire in her lungs, so she held her breath. Justīne lashed out, stabbing with Niklāvs' blade, goring Karīna's paw and wrist. Karīna swatted at her, but her body was slick with blood, and she dropped Justīne.

She fell through the darkness, praying to the Gods. She didn't know how far or even what she prayed for, only that she fell for longer than she'd expected. She couldn't see the ground through the darkness. For a moment Justīne was weightless, a cool wind at her back.

Then the ground rushed up to meet her. She heard something crack and a sharp pain shot through her ribs. She wanted to scream, but she had no air in her lungs. She breathed in deeply instead. As she did, wheezing, Justīne realized that she could just barely see the light of the sun. She'd fallen on the bank of the river, her top half in the light, everything below her waist submerged. The edge of the maalkonis stung her face and arms, discoloring her skin and leaving pale scars, but the parts of her body that were underwater seemed mostly untouched. The river rolled over her legs, cool water stinging her wounds. Niklāvs' blade had landed behind her. She stared at it and listened to the way shouting mixed with the droning atstrumeters and the pop of the guards' arquebuses. She couldn't see where they were firing.

Karīna landed beside her. She saw the feathered beast's glaring violet eyes, heard her growling and the violent rustle of her wings, all of it filled with malice. Justīne scrambled up the shore and grabbed Niklāvs' blade just before she was dragged back into the dark, pulled through the river. Water choked her throat, and river stones cut her back before she emerged on the other side—within the maalkonis once again. Justīne held her breath and gripped the blade tight. The maalkonis burned her and stung her eyes. Karīna lunged at Justīne, her jaws wide and fangs bared, as Justīne thrust the blade into her throat.

Karīna froze as black blood dripped from the wound, and violet light spread across her like the fissures in the oak. Justīne stabbed again, aiming for her heart this time. More violet fissures spread out through her body, and her scales began to crack. Again Justīne stabbed, and the light grew brighter, the cracks wider. Justīne's grip was slippery with black blood.

"I'm sorry," Justīne cried, her throat and lungs stinging. Tears ran down her cheeks. "I had no choice."

Karīna's bones began to break and shift. Feathers fell off of her, and the violet color in her eyes dimmed until they became a cool blue. She looked mortified, exhausted, almost human. Karīna's expression softened, though tears streamed from her eyes. As the maalkonis rushed toward them—into them—Karīna made a quick series of signs with her clawed hands, bright violet light trailing in the air, forming a violet rune. Justīne recognized the shape of it: 'gust.'

All at once, a mystical wind emanated from Karīna, and a gap appeared between them and the bridge to The Old Town. The winds tossed Justīne through the opening with such great force that her body soared over the copper bridge. She collapsed on the other side, green grass catching in her mouth. Justīne heard Anna and the others shout as she landed.

When she looked up, the maalkonis had filled the space where she'd just stood. By the river, where the maalkonis was kept at bay, Justīne could see Karīna's bloody arm in the water, unmoving, dripping grey and pink into the current. The violet veins in her arm had expanded like a brittle piece of stone. The maalkonis did not rush toward her. Even in the cavity Anna had made when they charged in to try and save Karīna, the gap wasn't closing in. The dark clouds simply flowed around it.

Epilogue

Although a few voices among the rebellion had been the loudest and most effective at inciting it, they had had no true leadership or organization. Loyal members of the guard had joined other brave Ļaodil, and together they'd regrouped, formed a front in the south, and steadily regained control of The Old Town. The bloody work had taken all noctis.

They'd worked hard to capture the rebels—there were too few people left in the world to kill so many. However, there had been several casualties among those who'd refused to be put in chains, and among the wounded, there had been too many for Sofija to treat on her own.

The Lord Mayor had been struck down in battle, though nobody was sure who dealt the final blow. The Lord Mayor's wife, Beatrice, had declared Ievan and Lilija traitors to the town and the Gods alike. They were, after all, the two who had sown the most doubt and spurred the violence. She'd had them both executed.

Ievan had chosen to walk into the maalkonis, while Lilija had chosen the sword. They had both been killed in the early light of first dim, mere minutes before Justīne, Anna, and Gustavs had arrived.

As much as Justīne despised them for what they did, The Old Town felt a little emptier without the traitors. Even so, she did not mourn their lives—except that she wished she'd been the one to kill Ievan. Instead, he'd taken the easy way out, and Justīne had been forced to fight Karīna instead.

Justīne spent a great deal of time in the days after they returned wondering if she could have done anything different, often waking up in a terror. She dreamed of arquebuses firing, blades clashing, the cathedral burning, and of fighting Karīna in the monstrous form that the maalkonis had changed her into. Had that really been her best chance at survival? Would they have been able to carry her to Sofija in time for her to remove the arquebus ball and bind the wound? Justīne struggled between consoling herself that they'd done everything they could to help her and wondering if they'd accidentally killed her.

Meanwhile, things returned to normal; in so far as the days could possibly be *normal* anymore, with each family returning to their regular jobs. Once, when Sofija came to check on Justīne's wounds, they spoke about how strange it was that, after everything, people just went back to their lives. The surgeon smiled and said, "The Ļaodil understand one thing better than all others: work. It is what keeps us alive in this dark world and what calms our nerves."

"Is that a good thing?" Justīne asked.

"Sometimes," Sofija said. "Other times, I am not so sure."

Sofija, Dādi, and other visitors helped to catch up Justīne on what was happening around town while she rested. Justīne had never heard such delicious gossip: the late Lord Mayor Dmitraj had been stockpiling ale, and his wife was fully in her cups every night; Krišs had apparently snuck some of Lilija's chickens into a makeshift coop (a closet) in the dead of noctis (a guard found and removed the birds); and Bruno was sleeping with Aleks' daughter. Apparently, they'd fought each other during the rebellion and had a hard time getting their hands off each other after it was over. Justīne could hardly wrap her head around what compelled them to such extremes. By way of explaining it, Sofija simply said, "I don't understand why you don't understand. They're both *very* attractive. Given the opportunity, well..." She bit her lip, and they both laughed.

Dādi and Ešlija visited daily, fretting over her health and making sure she ate. Only after Justīne reassured them that she was recovering well—dozens of times—they would bring news from The Old Town. Ešlija was helping the new Lord Mayor, Beatrice, by overseeing trials for those who had supported the rebellion and survived the fighting. Each of the accused was given a chance to work off their sins under the watch of the town's guards. The nature of their work and the duration of their oversight varied based on how they'd conducted themselves in the battle. Some, such as Ievan's apprentice, seemed to have been dragged in against his will. Others had taken to it gleefully, so much so that Ešlija said it was hard to look them in the eye.

It was difficult, but to do anything else would spell the end of numerous professions and the loss of so much unwritten knowledge. With the existing casualties and executions, those who remained were already struggling to fill their shoes. Beatrice's decision to reintegrate some of those who'd reveled in the fighting was unpopular, but she argued any more deaths would spell the end of The Old Town.

Dādi was still devastated that the creature Ešlija shot was Karīna. He refused to discuss it for several days. He insisted that he didn't fault her—he claimed he would have fired the arquebus had he been the one holding it. Justīne suspected that might have been what tore him up the most.

What he did speak of—and often—was Anna's atstru-torch. He desperately wanted to understand it, but Justīne had few answers for her, and Anna hadn't spoken to him since that day. She'd taken up residence in Monika's old home. She organized the books that the woman had left behind and began making more atstru-torches. When Dādi offered to help, she refused.

Dādi told her about how Anna carved out a small piece of the maalkonis once her torch was recharged, revealing Karīna and Ievan's corpses. Justīne was able to attend the funeral, hobbling down the hill with Anna's help. Gustavs stood beside them, and for the first time, Justīne saw the burns on his body. They were still red and healing. His arm bore stitches where Karīna had wounded him.

Karīna and Ievan burned in a pyre, their ashes ascending into the heavens as Sofija and Staņislavs sang, and Justīne's heart felt just a bit lighter. She prayed that the woman had found the Bright Garden.

As for Ievan, she wished nothing but the worst for that murderer. Even the Hell of Ends was too good for him. It had been a week since he'd chased them out of The

Old Town, and she still dreamt of finding poor Niklāvs collapsed against her front door. Anna had come by to clean his blood off her door, but Justīne could still find traces of it. The mere mention of Ievan's name still put the taste of blood and ash in her mouth. She spat, snow melting where her saliva landed.

As Justīne began to return to work around the farm, preparing for spring, Sofija's brother Staņislavs arrived one day with a lovely cane for her. He'd carved it himself from an oak tree. Somebody had told him about the giant oak in the maalkonis, so he'd been adamant that the cane be made from a similar tree, even if it was a regular oak. Justīne hated that she needed it at all, but using the cane was preferable to stumbling around the fields on her own. Besides, it was beautifully made. Staņislavs had even carved Pūka's face into the horn. He showed the cat when he delivered it, who rubbed up against it and purred. He laughed, a light and airy sound. Justīne lost count of how many times she'd thanked him.

Anna created another atstru-torch. When Gustavs recovered from his wounds, he used it to lead a party out to the ancient oak tree to collect more of its sap as well as a few acorns so that they could try to plant more trees like it. It would take many years to pay off, if it did at all, but Justīne was excited by the idea that they would have their own magical tree farm.

Gustavs was accompanied by four guards in case anything attacked from the maalkonis. Karīna's warnings about the mountains had been clear, so they went the long way through the mortežs. While they were there, he checked the pool to see if Karīna had revived in a new body, as she had when she fell in the caves. It was impossible to tell one way or another, but the water was only occupied by plants and rotting wood.

Anna remained hopeful, despite the news, but Justīne had seen the woman's body burn. She was fairly confident that was the end of it. She would like to be proven wrong. The maalkonis was still out there, and they still didn't really understand how any of it worked. Not even Karīna had.

As the weeks went on, the quiet grudge Anna kept toward Dādi faded, and she eventually asked him to help with a new version of her atstru-torch. She was having trouble with a few cogs catching when they ran for too long. Evidently, they'd been much luckier than any of them had realized when they'd spent that day in the maalkonis. Dādi continued to work on the atstrumeters, but he spent every other moment working with Anna at her place. As he became more familiar with her atstru-torches, he found ways to not only fix the issues she'd been having but also help them burn brighter and improve the trigger mechanism.

Once they had enough torches, Anna taught a few people how to draw the arcane runes on them. Gustavs, Staņislavs, and Teodor became The Old Town's first *tumērnsa*—the first members of an expedition team. They were tasked with removing the maalkonis and mapping what lay hidden in it. The work was slow, but once they removed the maalkonis from an area, it did not return. After their first outing, Beatrice celebrated with a feast, which, considering the restrictions on their food stores, looked more like a fancy meal than a *feast*. But the Ļaodil seemed to appreciate it nonetheless. People drank, danced, and sang all through noctis—and for once the dark didn't seem quite so frightening.

Teodor, who had been very timid when he'd joined the team on account of the fact that he'd sided with Ievan and Lilija, quickly became fond of drawing maps of what they uncovered. He drafted them in the field then drew more readable versions at his desk back home. He seemed to take great pride in sharing them with the Ļaodil, as if he saw redemption in the ink and parchment. Perhaps it was, because even Beatrice, who still held a deep grudge toward those who participated in the failed rebellion, seemed to value his work. She used his maps to help plan The Old Town's expansion, because suddenly they'd found themselves in the unusual situation where they could move beyond the old brick walls.

Justīne had no interest in going anywhere near the maalkonis again, even with a torch. Her body still hadn't recovered from her fight with Karīna, and Sofija had made it clear that some of her wounds would never fully go away. Her burns and cuts had mostly healed, but she still walked with a limp, and pain had become a constant companion. She took the cane that Staņislavs carved for her everywhere, and she became a regular visitor of Sofija's, who prescribed her a variety of poultices and oils that helped make breathing a bit more comfortable.

Justīne once asked Anna if there was anything that she could do, since she was learning the runes in Monika's and Karīna's books. With the quick lessons she'd gotten from the latter, and understanding rune pairing, things were coming to her more easily. She would occasionally cast a spell to help other people with their own problems if she could, boiling some water to purify it for Bruno and summoning ice to cool one of Ešlija's drinks.

"There are mending runes in Monika's books," Anna said, "but she's written that they are extremely dangerous. I've never even tried them. I imagine that one mistake could have major consequences: a bone growing in the wrong place, muscles healing the wrong way…"

"I understand," Justīne said. She was disappointed, but it was the answer she had expected.

"I'll try to practice the signs when I can, though," Anna added. "If I can learn them and make sure they're safe enough, maybe I can help."

Staņislavs began visiting her more often. Seeing him was the best part of Justīne's days. For a fleeting moment, her doubts and worries quieted, and they simply spent time together, exchanging stories and dreams. One noctis, they stared up at a large white shape suspended in the sky. Sometimes it was only a sliver, other times a massive orb, but so long as it was there, it always gave off a white haze. They were both familiar with the trickle of light, but neither of them had ever seen the source through the darkness. As the maalkonis around them became cleared, the silvery thing began to show its face. Justīne told him the name that Karīna had given it during that noctis when she was in the maalkonis—*mūnes*.

Justīne knew that he wanted more from her, but the closer they got, the more she thought of Niklāvs. She didn't understand it. It wasn't as if they had even been that close, and yet she couldn't get the late guard or his words out of her mind. She tried to explain it to Staņislavs one day. She wasn't sure that he understood, but he didn't seem upset either. Disappointed, perhaps, but not upset.

"I think I understand," he said. "Kind of. When the rebellion happened… Well, I watched one of them cleave through a guard's stomach. Tore things out of him that I wish I could unsee. I can't even remember his name, but the memories come back when I least expect it—while awake and in my dreams." He balled a fist, and for the first time Justīne saw fury build in his amber eyes. "Beatrice has been too lenient on them. I know we need their help to keep The Old Town running, but sometimes I wish they'd met Ievan and Lilija's fate instead."

Justīne reached out and touched his hand. "Me too. But they—many of them—are trying to atone. Teodor, for example. I hear he's been helpful on your expeditions."

Staņislavs nodded. "Yeah. He's alright. He was just led down the wrong path is all. His father's kind of an ass."

Justīne laughed. "I don't think Krišs has ever said a word to me. Well, maybe *a* word, but certainly never a kind one."

After he left, Pūka stared at her, blinking silently. It was moments like that when she was glad the cat couldn't *actually* speak. She was certain the cat was judging her, and not favorably. "What is it this time?" she asked Pūka. "Are you upset that Staņislavs and I wished ill upon the traitors, or am I late to feeding you?"

Pūka purred, watching her.

Sometimes—and she would never admit this to Pūka—she missed talking with her. Even if it hadn't truly been Pūka speaking.

The expeditions that Gustavs, Staņislavs, and Teodor carried out slowly morphed into rescue missions. They began to discover other people lost to the maalkonis, warped into beasts the same way Karīna had been. Anna made it her mission—and thus the mission of their expansion—to save as many people as they could. Sometimes they were successful. Other times they simply put up too much of a fight. It was difficult work, but it gave the Ļaodil hope in a way that simply wasn't possible before.

Justīne took on two apprentices to help serve the growing needs of The Old Town. She was relieved for the help. Some things were simply too difficult with her wounds. Especially as spring rolled around, she found it difficult to work at the pace she needed, and she no longer had the strength to plow the fields. Zigmārs was her first apprentice, Lord Mayor Beatrice's son. He was eager to learn and loved to hear stories about how Justīne and her siblings defeated the maalkonis. He was a good kid, though Justīne felt uncomfortable with the way he seemed to revere her sometimes.

The second was one of the lost who Staņislavs had helped bring back from the maalkonis, a woman who couldn't remember her own name after so long in the dark. After some time, when it was clear her memory of it was gone, she named herself Filomena.

Filomena had tended farms before the dark took her. She and Justīne would sit around a fire some nocti and share what they knew. Every day, Filomena seemed to remember more, and their relationship gradually shifted from a mentorship to a partnership. Between what she learned from Graudiņš and the memories that Filomena recovered, they were able to help one another.

When the expansion pushed far enough and the land began to heal, Filomena began working new fields along the river, on a narrow strip of land south of The Old Town's walls. They still met up sometimes, but not quite as often. Justīne was just glad that she no longer bore the weight of feeding everyone alone.

Beatrice gave up the mayorship after a year and returned to her bakery. Staņislavs suggested that Justīne run for the office. He was insistent that she would be perfect for the role, flattering her with all kinds of compliments. She told him that she couldn't imagine running The Old Town—and at the age of eighteen, no less. "Nobody would take me seriously," she insisted.

"But they already already do," Staņislavs said, shrugging the way he did when he thought the argument was over.

Ešlija won the vote. Thanks to her time on patrol and how she had helped Beatrice in the prior year, she'd gotten to know everybody well. The election was mostly a formality. She had no real contestants. Justīne had gotten a few votes, probably thanks to Staņislavs' meddling. Aleks had gotten second place, but he didn't seem particularly upset when he lost. He and Beatrice became Ešlija's most frequent advisors—who she went to when she needed another perspective on matters.

Justīne visited Anna's home one midday during the following summer. The scent of rain and muddy earth filled the air, and the maalkonis had receded enough that the sky shone vibrantly and blue over the center of The Old Town. A few months prior, she would have remarked on how unusual it was, but each day, that sight was becoming more commonplace.

Justīne knocked on the door, though she was sure the pounding of her cane had already made her sister aware of her presence. Anna invited her inside, and she sat in a wicker chair. Anna poured their ale into a pair of copper cups.

"It's a new flavor," she said. "Bruno gave me some to try. He called it *medustums*. Something like that. I guess his new apprentice, that boy they found out west in the mortežs, came up with it. I love how sweet it is."

It was indeed sweet. At first, more so than she liked, but on the second sip, Justīne began to take a liking to the ale.

"This is dangerous." Justīne laughed.

"Isn't it?" Anna asked, taking the seat beside her.

"So," Justīne said, "what was it you wanted to tell me?"

"Oh, right! So, Dādi and I have been working on the atstru-torches—he came up with a better name for them, actually. He calls them *beacons*. Like for helping the lost find their way back. I don't know; I like it. Much easier to say than *atstru-torch*. I don't know why I didn't think of it."

"Anna."

"Anyway, we made a new type of beacon. It does all the stuff a better beacon should. It lasts longer, is more resilient—you know. But this is the exciting part: I had Gustavs try it out yesterday, and he said that—and I quote—it 'ripped the maalkonis right out of a creature.'"

"Wasn't the old torch—beacon—doing that?"

"Not to this degree. I think what the first one did to Karīna and the others had hurt and weakened them. It might have helped her recover, but this thing saps the dark right from a person and returns them to their natural body like that." She snapped, the ale in her cup spilling over the rim of her cup. She didn't seem to notice it. "Well, not *like that*. It still takes some time. The one Gustavs tried it on still had time to run away, but this is a game-changer. The tumērnsa teams will have a much easier time helping those they find out there."

"Teams? Multiple?"

"Yeah. Dādi is almost finished with the second beacon. Once we have a few more, we plan to create a second expedition team. It will take some time, we don't have many people to spare, but I've already spoken about it with Ešlija. One of the guards she used to work with has already volunteered to lead it. Once that's ready, and they've learned the runes they'll need, they'll start clearing out the west. We might even be able to regrow the forest out that way, where the mortežs is. It would take time, obviously, but Ešlija is keen to plant a new forest soon. She's worried about the north part of town and the wood we need to fuel our hearths through winter."

"Makes sense," Justīne said. "It's wild how much things have changed. You and Ešlija are expanding The Old Town, saving lives."

"It's not just expansion. I mean, I guess it is in the short term, but this is *world-changing*. It's been months, and the maalkonis has barely recovered the ground it lost. You can see the sun in the sky. Not that dim light through the clouds, but you can actually see the sun now. I know we didn't set out to do any of this, but Justīne, we're gonna save the whole damned world."

Justīne frowned. "All of the stories about the world as it was, all the fighting and squabbling over resources, warring kingdoms and such... Do you think we're ready to deal with that?"

Anna shrugged. "As far as I can tell, that's us too. The rebellion last year happened because a few people wanted to be in charge of our food stores, right? Or, rather, so that you and the Lord Mayor *weren't* in charge. This might lead to different problems, but they aren't new ones."

Justīne took another sip from her cup, unconvinced.

"Don't you worry, June," Anna reassured her. "This is just the start."

They stayed together through most of the day, until last dim approached, and Justīne's joints began to ache. She stopped by Sofija's place to get something for the pain and then made the long walk back to her farmhouse. Along the way, Justīne saw children, some of them among the rescued lost, playing in the streets. Her apprentice, Zigmārs, was at the training ring. He was practicing with a sword alongside Gustavs, as she used to do. Aleks was telling a story to some of the guards, recounting what he'd seen at first dim that day Justīne had returned from the maalkonis. And Krišs leaned against his butchery, grimacing while he whittled a piece of oak. Even in his solitary grumpiness, there was a kind of peace.

Justīne ascended the hill, leaving them behind her, relishing the quiet of the farm. But, also, her heart was full, excited to see what Anna would do next. She had no idea what her sister was capable of, nor what the world might look like by winter. In a year's time. However long would it take for the forests to grow back and the rivers to run clear. One day, perhaps, they reach the vast pools of salt water that the legends spoke of. If they were really out there. It was all so difficult to imagine.

Pūka found her sitting alone at the kitchen table. She leapt up on Justīne's lap, kneaded her legs, clawing into her breeches painfully, but soon settled there. In minutes, Justīne could hear the damned cat snoring peacefully. She sat there for a while, careful not to move so she didn't disturb Pūka's rest. Justīne glanced out the window, looking out across the town, and wondered if Staņislavs would find any other cats among those lost in the maalkonis.

Acknowledgements

Firstly, thank you for reading *Copper Skin, Oaken Lungs!* I had a lot of fun with this story, and I hope you enjoyed it as well. If you have the time, please consider leaving a book a review wherever you purchase or discuss your latest reads. They're a massive help!

Thanks to Maggie Hoopis, Steven Raaymakers, and Emory Glass for their early feedback on this story. Also to my ARC team for taking a chance on this story. Additional thanks to my fantastic editors, Ed Crocker and Qilanna Quinn.

Finally, thanks to Silvia Gorchakova, who illustrated this book's amazing cover art.

The original idea for *Copper Skin, Oaken Lungs* came from listening to "Bur man laimi" by Tautumeitas over and over again. Their album, *Zem Saules / Under the Solar Spell*, kept me company while I worked on this. I highly recommend checking it out.

Also… Justīne, Anna, and Gustavs will return in a new adventure.

About the Author

Adam Bassett is an author, designer, and illustrator originally from northern New York. He is also the author of the cyberpunk series *Digital Extremities* and the reference book *An Author's Guide to Setting Design: Worldbuilding & Cartography.*

His work has also been published in anthologies such as *Rare* (Alex Parker Publishing), and *Nature Erupts* (Two Doctors Media). He previously volunteered as the Editor-in-Chief at Worldbuilding Magazine.

Visit adamcbassett.com to see more of his work and subscribe to his newsletter for updates. You can also follow Adam on Bluesky, Instagram, or Threads.

Content Warnings

Copper Skin, Oaken Lungs contains some descriptions of violence and scenes which may bother people with nyctophobia or claustrophobia.